THE KILLERS OF INNOCENCE

JOHN CREASEY

THE KILLERS OF INNOCENCE

A DOCTOR PALFREY THRILLER

WALKER AND COMPANY
New York

First published in the United States of America in 1971 by the Walker Publishing Company, Inc.

Published simultaneously in Canada by Fitzhenry & Whiteside, Limited, Toronto.

ISBN: 0-8027-5234-9

Library of Congress Catalog Card Number: 71-161113

Printed in the United States of America from type set in the United Kingdom.

Contents

1

Dr. Palfrey is Bored

'SAP,' said Drusilla Palfrey to her husband, 'don't look like that, or you'll cause an international incident.'

Dr. Alexander Stanislaus Palfrey's expression turned to one of open despair.

'Never allow me to come to a reception in Paris again, Drusilla. It isn't worth it, even for the food. Aren't we ever going to dance?' Palfrey took Drusilla's hand in his, toying with the single solitaire diamond of her engagement ring, and the plain gold of her wedding ring. 'Would you like an ice cream?'

'No,' said Drusilla. 'Darling, who would you say is the most beautiful woman here?'

'You, fisher-lady.'

'Be serious for a moment. I want to know.'

Palfrey's gaze roamed lazily round the great ballroom. Next morning, the newspapers would describe the scene as one of glittering splendour and would wax ecstatic about the dresses and the jewellery. The newspapers would also give prominence to the activities, marriages and hobbies, past present and future, of the great ones of several lands. They might, if they were allowed sufficient space by their editors, even mention Dr. Palfrey and his wife. If they were able to give the Palfreys four lines, instead of an honourable mention, they would probably describe him as the world Secret Service Ace; of late they had used the word 'ace' about him often. There would be photographs in the glossy weeklies of London, Paris, Rome, Brussels and, perhaps, even New York, but it was unlikely that the Palfreys would be pictured among the gallery of Excellencies, minor royalties, dukes and duchesses.

Palfrey's gaze stopped roving.

Sitting not far away from him a woman was leaning forward and touching the arm of a distinguished-looking, bearded man. She was dressed in scarlet velvet, her dark glossy hair swept high, with here and there the scintillating fire of diamonds. She was deep bosomed, and magnificently formed, yet it was her eyes which fascinated. At a distance of several yards, they gave to a beautiful face a vitality which made her stand out among everyone else.

'I *thought* so,' said Drusilla. 'I'd like to meet her, Sap.'

'Do I know anyone in her group?' mused Palfrey, and glanced from man to man; there were only two other women in a group of seven. 'No—no—no—but he looks familiar Where have I seen that beard before? Definitely hidalgoish, and they're both Spanish, or I miss my guess.'

'Do you know him?'

'His Excellency the Duke of Alga, I think. One-time Ambassador to London and to Paris, a cultured gent with a marvellous knack of getting on the right horse at the right time. He became a Falangist with about ten seconds to spare, and was used at once by the Caudillo. Just back from Buenos Aires, where, I understand, he got along famously with Madame Peron. Why are you so curious?'

Drusilla laughed.

'Any interest shown by one's escort is better than none, and must be encouraged.'

'Oh, well,' said Palfrey. 'Did I look as bored as that? I met Alga last year, during the little spot of bother we had in South America. Sure you don't mind being left alone?'

'A hundred to one that the Duke won't recognise you,' said Drusilla.

'Done! In kisses.' Palfrey stood up, and revealed himself as a tall, lean man, with slightly rounded shoulders, silky fair hair and a curious ease of movement. He was resplendent in a dress suit, modestly garnished with miniature medals.

In the vast room, two thousand people had already gathered; the banquet was over, the dancing not yet begun. As Palfrey neared the table where the group of seven was sitting, the members of the orchestra took their places on a platform on the far side of the room.

The Duke of Alga, his pale hand toying with his little dark grey beard, was dressed in the full regalia of a rank which Palfrey did not recognise. As the band started, he stood up and approached Palfrey.

The beauty with the wonderful eyes looked on as punctilious civilities were exchanged. Presently she accepted Palfrey's request to dance with him.

There was little subsequent opportunity for the Palfreys to talk of her, for friends gathered round them, champagne flowed, and the dance went long into the night.

It was not until five o'clock in the morning that, in their modest hotel in the Champs Elysées, Palfrey knelt to take off his wife's golden slippers.

'Like some tea?'

'Let me get into bed first.' Drusilla made no attempt to get up. 'Well, what do you think of her?'

'At the moment, not bad. In ten years' time, probably fifteen stone and unwieldly with it.'

'Now you've overdone it,' said Drusilla. 'She's quite the loveliest woman I've ever seen, and I'm almost sure that you have.'

'Nonsense!'

'Liar,' repeated Drusilla, lazily.

'Cross my heart.'

Drusilla opened her eyes wider, and looked at him as if she were seeing him for the first time. He stood back, smiling, enjoying the picture she made; it was one of the moments when he fully appreciated his great good fortune in the fact that she was still in love with him. They had been married for over ten years, and his prayer was that such love would last as long as life itself.

'I really begin to believe you,' said Drusilla. 'So you didn't notice her looking at you, and asking who you were?'

He shook his head, smiling, not really believing her.

'I'm too comfortable to move,' she said, as he lit a cigarette. 'Thanks, darling. You go to bed.'

'And have to get out again, to unhook or unzip you? Sweetheart, listen. Such things have happened. I'm a Secret Service chief. Nothing really surprising even in a Señora's interest.'

'She is a widow,' said Drusilla, unkindly.

'Really!'

'With three children— two girls and a boy.'

'Indeed!'

'She is staying in Paris for four days.'

'Well, well! So are we.'

'We are having tea with her tomorrow afternoon at Rumpelmayer's. Darling I haven't taken leave of my senses, she was really interested in you. I didn't suggest meeting again, she did. If Alga hadn't been able to waylay you then, he would have found some other way. No, she didn't say so, but I gathered it.'

'The psychic wife. Strange you didn't spy in your little crystal ball that I have an appointment at the Embassy tomorrow afternoon.'

'Postpone it,' said Drusilla. 'Tell them that you have unearthed another deadly plot, and have to see the siren who's mixed up in it. They will believe anything of the great Alexander. Darling, *do* help me off with my dress.'

'You know,' said Palfrey, thoughtfully, 'I believe you're serious about this business.'

'I am,' Drusilla said drowsily. 'You see, darling, she came here to see you this afternoon. I forgot to tell you. We were out, and when I came in, the receptionist told me that she had been asking for you. *Not* for us. She didn't leave her name.'

'Then how do you know——' began Palfrey.

'She left as I came in, and the receptionist told me she had only just gone out. Even I couldn't mistake Señora Melano for anyone else, could I?'

'I suppose not,' conceded Palfrey.

Drusilla did not speak again, and soon he heard her even breathing; she had a trick of dropping off to sleep, sometimes in the middle of a sentence. He stared at the ceiling, frowning; she had driven sleep away from him, and a dozen thoughts were floating in his mind, none of them definite. He knew of no reason why the woman should want to see him.

10

In his work, serious, even perilous events could burgeon from the most insignificant beginnings. His life, he thought, was like a simmering kettle which might bubble up to boiling point with little or no warning.

He moved restlessly from side to side until, finally, he slept.

2

Tête-à-tête

SHE WORE a black suit, superbly tailored, with lines which Palfrey knew intuitively would excite Drusilla's envy. Even if her suit failed to do that, her hat most certainly would. To call it 'wide' would have been to show a dismal lack of imagination. It had a vast brim, and was tilted so that one side almost touched her shoulder, and the other revealed her lovely profile and her dark, blue-black hair. She walked, several minutes after Palfrey, through the shadowy seclusion of Rumpelmayer's. Meeting him her eyes lit up; then clouded.

'But your wife, Dr. Palfrey?'

'Delayed,' Palfrey said. 'Terribly sorry, but there was a telephone call from London. Some slight indisposition of one of the children; a temperature, anyhow. My wife will come if the report is all clear, but will send a message if she can't make it.'

'I'm so dreadfully sorry,' said Señora Melano.

'Oh, it'll be nothing.'

'You men, you are so calm about it,' she said.

'A different sense of proportion, perhaps. Let's order tea and go along and choose some cakes. I'm told they have some of those whipped cream things.'

She laughed.

'You are so lean, you can eat cream and more cream and not an inch to the bad!'

The waitress took their order for tea, while Señora Melano tried again, unconvincingly, to pretend that she was sorry they were alone.

She poured out.

'Tell me,' she said, handing him his cup, 'in your work, are you very often afraid?'

'Often. Terrified!'

'Please, be serious.'

'I am serious.'

'So,' she said, 'you understand fear.' She leaned back and looked at him, as if trying to decide whether he was telling the truth. 'Will you believe that I am frightened?'

Palfrey didn't speak.

'Not for myself,' she said, 'and yet perhaps . . . for myself. Harm to my children would be despair, for me.'

Palfrey did nothing to encourage her, waiting patiently for the mystery to unravel.

'I am frightened, for them,' she went on. 'Dr. Palfrey, you are an astute man, you have much experience, you could perhaps help me in the strange . . . what you say? . . . predicament. Four days ago, when I was about to leave Madrid for Paris, my Fesina was . . . taken away.' Her voice was steady, now, but animation had gone from her face. 'I was . . . distraught. She had been to a party, with other children, left with them . . . and did not come back. Her duenna was ill, and Anita, my other daughter in charge. Being but fifteen, she was not perhaps as astute as an older girl would have been.'

Rumpelmayer's, the people, the soft-footed waitresses, the murmur of conversation, all faded. Palfrey was aware of himself and the woman. No other.

Her voice was pitched low, her English becoming more broken.

'In two days, I was without calm. What is your word . . . frantic. My friend the Duke, he helps. The police, the army, everyone looks. Perhaps you read about it?'

'I don't read the Spanish newspapers,' Palfrey said.

'All of them, it was in big letters. I expect to find her dead, perhaps. Hurt. Ill-treated. Then she return. She escaped. She remembers . . . little. A small letter, saying so much and saying so little.'

Her hands, until then resting in her lap, were moving, the

13

fingers intertwining; her right hand was bare, the left was gloved; black and white vied with each other in a changing pattern.

'Yes,' murmured Palfrey.

'It says this, Dr. Palfrey. *"It can happen again. It will happen again. You will obey".*' She paused, and when he did not speak, raised her right hand and clenched it on the table. 'But what do I obey? Nothing! I have no orders, no requests, it is the complete mystery. Yet I can see that letter, so very clear: *"It can happen again. It will happen again. You will obey".* And now . . . I am frightened. Perhaps they send me an order and I have not received it. Then Fesina . . .' she broke off. 'I have two guards, to watch the children, night and day. Nothing can happen to them, and yet I am afraid of that which cannot happen. Do you understand?'

'I think so,' murmured Palfrey. 'I shouldn't worry, yet. If they have a message for you, it will reach you. They'll make no mistake about it.'

'I try to tell myself that, but——'

'I know,' said Palfrey. 'The worst seems always likely when you have children. Don't worry, Señora. What has the Duke said about this message?'

She looked away.

'He will help?' asked Palfrey.

She looked up, the beauty framed in that great hat hurtful in its perfection. The glowing eyes, wracked as if with pain, the superb complexion, the lips, parted just a little, seemed part of a picture painted by a great artist.

'I did not tell him.'

Palfrey considered, and then asked: 'Why?'

He sipped his tea, trying, by that small, domestic act, to bring her back to normality.

'Why?' repeated Palfrey.

'He has so much anxiety,' said Señora Melano. 'That . . . and more Dr. Palfrey. I am not a rich woman, I have much expense. I tell you this, to my embarrassment, but I think I should tell you, because I want your help. This dress . . . all my clothes . . . I am but a mannequin. My children and my household cost so much, and my husband died a poor man. That is known, to some. I am not ashamed of it among my

14

friends, and the gossips . . .' she shrugged her shoulders, a superb gesture of disdain . . . 'they do not matter. But some weeks ago, I was made an offer.'

Palfrey said: 'By whom?'

He was aware that Drusilla had come in, that she was standing some distance away, sensing that it would be a bad moment to interrupt. He looked only at the Spanish woman.

'I do not know. I was promised much money . . . one thousand American dollars . . . for some information I could obtain, from . . . the Duke.'

'Ah,' said Palfrey, and the sound was like a sigh.

'You understand?' She was swift. 'I put two together. I refused . . .' her gesture of scorn was quick and compelling. 'I do not tell secrets, but . . . Dr. Palfrey, for my children, I will do . . . anything.' She whispered the last word, and a different expression stole into her face; defiant daring, determined.

'I see,' said Palfrey, gently. 'I think perhaps you should.'

'*Should?*' she breathed.

'In principle,' said Palfrey. He looked up, and saw Drusilla's back, as she went out; she turned at the door, caught sight of him, and smiled; there was only one Drusilla, only one woman with that complete understanding. He smiled at the thought and dismissed her from his mind. 'Only in principle! Señora Melano, what can I do?'

'I am not sure. I have, of course, heard much of you. The Duke told me of the miracle in South America, when you saved us all from catastrophe. I have always wondered what you were like.' She gave a little laugh. 'I did not expect to find out, like this. Dr. Palfrey, it is reasonable to suppose I shall be ordered to obtain secret information from the Duke. Information about, perhaps, the defence plans of my country. I am to be made—a *spy.*'

She sat back; and looked as if that were all she need say, as if the little word would explain everything that Palfrey wanted to know.

He said: 'And I hunt spies.'

'Do you not?'

'Oh, yes,' said Palfrey. 'Yes. There would be one way to buy safety for your children, Señora.'

'How?'

15

'To obtain this information, if they ask for it.'

'*You* say that, you who——'

'It need not be accurate information,' murmured Palfrey. 'Official looking, genuine in appearance, but . . .' he shrugged. 'It could be arranged. You would, of course, allow an agent to follow you, to see where you had to send the information.'

'Yes, yes, anything!' Her eyes glowed. 'But will the Duke——'

'It can be arranged.' Palfrey was almost brusque. 'Tell me more about the disappearance of Fesina. She was with the other children——'

'With a party, yes. In all, nine. She and another child disappeared together.'

'How old is Fesina?'

'Eleven,' said the Señora, simply.

Palfrey smiled encouragingly, and sat upright. 'Let's order some more tea. Everything can be arranged——'

She was subdued in her gratitude; perhaps not quite certain that it would be as easy as he imagined.

Prince Carel, adored son of the third woman in the Netherlands, was a problem child. At the age of ten, he showed signs of developing a craze for speed and a wanderlust which, three times in six months, set the newspaper headlines quivering through the ether even over such refined wavelengths as those used by the British Broadcasting Corporation.

After each occasion Prince Carel returned to the Palace unharmed. At the time of the third escapade, he was no more than eleven, and for the six following months, he was such a model of rectitude that his guardians, believing him to have at last outgrown his wilfulness, relaxed their vigilance and allowed him to roam at will in the woods outside The Hague. It was here he was seen, on the morning of the day when Dr. Palfrey talked at Rumpelmayer's with Señora Melano, innocently playing in the company of another boy.

That night the young Prince did not return home to the Palace.

On the same morning, the young daughter of the Grand Duke of Nordia, was walking with her governess and two companions along the border of the great lake at Stockholm.

The governess, pausing to talk for a minute with a young man who had lately claimed her attention, allowed her charges to walk on, alone, to the jetty. Here they were hailed by two lads scarcely older than themselves, manning a small yacht.

When the governess turned to call them, they were aboard, sailing rapidly away from the shore.

The yacht did not return.

3

Dr. Palfrey Reads a Newspaper

DRUSILLA sat on the balcony outside her bedroom. It was cooler now than it had been during the day, for the sun had sunk behind the tall, terraced houses that lined the street. To the right she could glimpse the green boughs of a chestnut tree; but her attention was neither held, nor deflected. It was nearly seven o'clock, and Palfrey had not returned from his tête-à-tête with the Señora.

Every time a car or a taxi turned into the street and delivered a passenger to the hotel, Drusilla peered down through the scrolls of the balcony, hoping to see the tall figure of her husband; but it was one minute past seven before she saw him.

He was walking along the far side of the road, reading a newspaper with great concentration.

He reached the pavement nearly opposite the entrance to the hotel, and stepped into the roadway. A taxi which had just swung round the corner scorched towards him.

For a terrifying second Drusilla leaned against the balcony, too frightened to cry out. She saw a flutter of the paper, and Palfrey jump backwards nimbly. The taxi passed, and now only the lurid comments of the driver, who leaned out of his cab to shout them, disturbed the serenity of the quiet street.

A page of the newspaper fluttered to the ground.

Palfrey glanced up at Drusilla, waved, and went after it; but the wind played a joke with him, and swept it into the road. As he stooped forward a luxurious Renault turning, with a silence surprising for a motor car in Paris, purred down upon him.

'Sap!' cried Drusilla.

He watched the car go over the newspaper, and when it had passed, went forward again to retrieve it. The last Drusilla saw of him then was as he folded the soiled sheet carefully and tucked it under his arm.

She turned from the balcony, and dropping into the chair, lay back. She heard the whirr of the lift; then nothing until Palfrey's key turned in the lock.

He came in, briskly, and flung his hat on to the bed.

'Hallo, my sweet! I——'

Then he saw her pallor, and went across to her, dropping on one knee. Drusilla looked at him without speaking, her breath coming in quick shallow gasps. He pressed her hand, then suddenly jumped up, went to a cupboard in a wardrobe, and took out a bottle of brandy and a glass. He poured a little, and took it to her.

'Doctor's orders,' he said, and put his arm round her shoulders, helping her to sit up.

'I thought——' she began huskily, and broke off.

He smiled, gently; it gave his face a charm which few people saw. His right hand strayed to his forehead, a gesture very usual to him in times of thought, as he watched her intently, waiting for her to go on.

'It looked as if you'd walk right into it,' she said 'Sap, don't do that again. I shan't always be there to shout.'

'Actually,' said Palfrey, 'I think I saw the car out of the corner of my eye. Both corners, in fact. You didn't happen to notice the number, did you?'

'Number!' cried Drusilla. 'Do you think I was in a state of mind to take *numbers*?'

'No, I suppose not. The paper blew up in my face, so I couldn't see. Old, blue Citroen, wasn't it, and I think it had an odd-coloured wing. Three black, one brown. It rattled like George Stephenson's Rocket!' He had not let the paper fall from his arm, and now took it away and held it up. 'A very interesting paper, tonight.'

'Damn the paper!'

'You're feeling better,' said Palfrey, fondly. 'Did you notice

19

what happened to that remarkable taxi?'

'I noticed what nearly happened to you.' Colour was returning to Drusilla's cheeks. 'What on earth is in that paper to make you day-dream like that?'

'News. Now let's talk about that taxi,' said Palfrey, still fingering a wisp of hair lying across his forehead. 'It turned into the street on the right side of the road and stuck to it—remember?'

'Well, the right side of the road is the right side, in Paris,' said Drusilla.

'For no apparent reason, it then swerved on to the left side, which is the wrong side for Paris. Oh, yes,' he went on, as Drusilla's expression altered again. 'It came right over. Now I was as safe as houses while it stayed where it should be, but in trouble when it swung across. Not a good driver—or a very good driver. His *argot* was magnificent, he would have convinced anyone that he came from Montmartre, where all the garages are. Well, some of them.'

Drusilla said sharply: 'What are you trying to say?'

'That he tried to run me down.'

'I don't believe it.'

'Nor would anyone else.'

'Paris taxi drivers are reckless, you can never rely——'

'Paris taxi drivers are the most slandered and nearly the most efficient in the world,' said Palfrey firmly. 'They do not swing across from right to left unless something is in the way. I was in the way: I say! Do you think the chap wanted to read my newspaper?'

Drusilla did not think that funny.

'Sap, do you mean this?'

'Not a shadow of doubt,' said Palfrey. 'Sorry, sweet. We are, as they say, at the beginning of events. Large events, I shouldn't wonder.'

Drusilla moved rather shakily to the newspaper, and picked it up; it was *Ce Soir*.

'Page 1,' said Palfrey.

Drusilla scanned it, and saw a headline about a certain Mr. Bevin, an honourable mention for a Mr. Truman and a Generalissimo named Stalin, a picture of a road race, a pronouncement on Germany by the French Foreign Minister, and a brief report of the disappearances of Prince Carel and the daughter of the Grand Duke of Nordia.

'The penny hasn't dropped,' said Drusilla. 'Has that woman turned your head?'

'Juanita? No, just put ideas into it. Which reminds me, I forgot to tell you all about Juanita Melano and her second daughter, Anita. Or is it Fesina?'

He talked on, almost casually, drawing a vivid picture.

He had not quite finished when Drusilla picked up *Ce Soir* and scanned the page again.

'You needn't have risked your life the second time, you could have bought another paper downstairs.'

'Begging the issue in masterly fashion. See what I mean?'

'If you see any connection between these three things, you must be——'

'Don't you?' Palfrey asked.

The silence in the room was hardly affected by noises from the street and the movement of people passing the door. Drusilla's gaze shifted towards the dressing-table, and the photographs of the young Alexander, aged six, and the young Marion, aged three, taken in the grounds of their country home in England. The photographer had been a genius; the children might have been in the room with them.

Palfrey said: 'Just in case, I've telephoned home, and had a word with Corny. He's going to stay there until we get back, he can work from there as easily as from London. I shouldn't think there's anything to fear, but . . .' he shrugged. 'I also asked for a report of any youngsters who've disappeared in the past few months—scions of noble families, diplomats, millionaires and what-not. I've a hazy feeling that there have been several, spaced out at intervals so that you'd hardly notice them. Of course, I may be quite crazy; I'd be sure I was crazy but for that taxi cab. Which reminds me——'

He went to the telephone.

In excellent French he asked for a number, had two minor altercations with the girl at the exchange, and finally spoke to a man who answered to the name of Marcel.

He listened, and chuckled.

'No, old chap, not tickets for the Folies Bergére, and nothing to do with your more exotic night clubs. I'm interested in taxis.' He winked at Drusilla. 'How many Citroen taxis with three black wings and one brown do you think there are in Paris? . . . Very few, that's what I'm hoping . . . Do you thing you could have a word with your devoted friends at the Sûreté Génêrale, and see if it's possible to find one? . . . And then come and have dinner with us, we're dining late . . . All right, we'll have dinner with you . . . Eight-thirty, sharp. Goodbye.'

He rang off.

'That means nine o'clock, I've never known him less than half an hour late for a social appointment. What it is, to have agents all over the world!' He chuckled again, went across to Drusilla, put his arm round her waist, and said: 'What about an instalment of that debt?'

'What debt?'

'Hundred to one, remember, because the Duke of Alga recognised me.'

She kissed him lightly on the cheek, then suddenly pressed close to him. Her lips were soft and passionate and insistent upon his; there was fear in the kiss.

She drew back.

'My dear,' said Palfrey gently, 'I didn't want to scare you, but we've always faced the truth.' He sat on the arm of a chair. 'The facts, as I see them, are that three children of highly placed people have been kidnapped within a week; one of the harassed parents has come to see me; and someone tried to run me down in a taxi. Not an original method of murder, but occasionally effective. The things could be connected.'

'I wish I'd never heard of the woman!'

'She would have found an excuse to meet us,' said Palfrey. 'Her determination to see me is one of the curious facts. I'd like to know more about Juanita Melano.'

Drusilla didn't speak.

Palfrey laughed. 'I've just time for a bath. Had yours?'

'Yes.'

'I won't be ten minutes.'

Drusilla changed into the little black dress that was just right for a quiet dinner at an exclusive restaurant in Paris.

Wherever Marcel Dubonnet took them, it would be exclusive. He was one of the most remarkable young men in Paris; eligible, adored by dozens, he had so far remained unattached. *Persona grata* with a host of Ministers, past and present, he could bring pressure to bear in the Chamber of Deputies, was a patron of the arts—even, it was rumoured, the black arts of depravity. In every way, he was an exciting young man.

He had one occupation about which few people had the slightest suspicion. Marcel, a secret agent? Nonsense! Such a suggestion, if made, would have been treated as a good joke.

In point of fact, he was, at that time, the leading French agent of a world Secret Intelligence organisation. The remarkable thing was that the world knew about that organisation, knew its title—the convenient one of Z5—knew Dr. Palfrey as its leader. It was also known that agents of wide experience from nearly every country in the world belonged to Z5—and gave it their allegiance. It was an organisation that had started among the Allies, during the war, and had now become an integral part of the struggle for world unity.

Because of its international character, it did not spy upon governments or government agents. There might be matters which came within its aegis, showing the newest aspect of the East-West struggle between titans. It placed these before a Council in which all nations concerned were represented.

There were other matters . . .

The affairs of nations were not the affairs of Z5; it was the tortuous and involved struggle against individuals and groups that came within its orbit. With the discovery of atomic power, the hydrogen bomb and bacteria of virulent and deadly effect, power could be placed in the hands of a few individuals. A group could blackmail, and groups had blackmailed nations, and attempted to blackmail the world, and would again. Some sought power for its own sake, some rebelled against the international system, some—and these were dangerous fanatics —who saw governments as the ruination of man, and struggled to upset them.

There had been the man who had tried to destroy the civilised world.*

The Man Who Shook The World tells this story.

Marcel Dubonnet was one of many French agents of Z5 who were not known to the general public or to the French Government—only to a few chosen officials. Z5 had been dubbed an international police force, or even an international detective force—a C.I.D. or an F.B.I. with the whole world as its territory. The nations had accepted its value, each contributing to the funds of Z5.

Of all this, Palfrey was the leader.

He had a gift, which none could explain, of keeping his strangely assorted men in amicable and loyal friendship. He had another gift, for organisation. And he had a third, which the fanciful called second sight. It was, in fact, the action of a highly intelligent and sensitive mind brought to bear on matters which seemed trifling, but might be significant.

It was one thing to be the wife of Sap Palfrey.

It was another, to be the wife of the leader of Z5.

Palfrey came out of the bathroom, wearing a singlet and trunks. Most people, seeing him stripped, were surprised at his muscular strength, for the impression he gave, when fully dressed, was one of almost extreme delicacy.

Drusilla had laid out his dinner suit.

'Wonderful,' said Palfrey. 'And I'm hungry, Juanita put me off my tea. Feeling better?'

'I've decided to suspend judgment.'

'That's the spirit! You look lovely enough to turn Marcel's head.' He dressed rapidly, and was ready at twenty minutes to nine. 'Shall we go downstairs for a drink, or have one sent up here?'

'Have one sent up,' said Drusilla. 'Marcel will come straight here.'

Palfrey rang for the waiter, ordered gin and Italian, looked at his watch and said:

'He's only a quarter of an hour late, so far. Pity we couldn't make it a foursome, with Juanita to keep him company. I say! Now there is an apple for his eye. Perhaps we'll fix it for luncheon tomorrow. Marcel's better than most at finding out if we're being fooled. Ah—the drinks.'

They had ordered two rounds.

The second had nearly gone, and it was twenty minutes past

nine, when Palfrey went to the window and looked out into the darkening night. Daylight still lingered. A few people were walking up and down the street, but Marcel Dubonnet was not one of them.

'He's always late,' Drusilla said from behind him, 'you said so yourself.'

'Nearly an hour,' said Palfrey. 'He's probably got himself locked up. I shouldn't have sent him to the Sûreté.' He forced a laugh.

The telephone bell rang.

Palfrey turned and reached the instrument in an instant, and although Drusilla had seen him move like that a thousand times, the speed of it still surprised her. Yet he lifted the telephone slowly, and put it to his ear as if he had all the time in the world.

'Dr. Palfrey,' he said.

'I have a call for you, sir.' The operator's English was excellent. 'One moment.' There was a pause, then Palfrey heard a noise on the line followed by a whispering voice, which it was hard to identify.

'Sap, is that you?'

'Yes,' said Palfrey, and Drusilla saw the warmth, the gay humanity, drain out of him, to be replaced by a man of steel.

'This is Marcel. Come, the garage at the corner of Rue Berthe, and——'

He broke off, gasping. A haunting, moaning sound travelled down the wire, followed by the sharp click of the receiver falling from his grasp.

4

The Taxi

DRUSILLA said: 'I'm coming.'

Palfrey said: 'You are not, my darling, you're going downstairs to dinner, and you're going to stay within sight of fifty or sixty people until I come back.'

'Sap——'

'There isn't time to argue,' Palfrey said. 'Come on.' He took her elbow and led her towards the door. But he did not open it immediately or quickly. He listened intently, then switched off the light in the room and opened the door slowly, his right hand in his pocket.

The passage was lighted, and empty.

'More imagination,' he said lightly.

'Sap, this isn't a job for you. One of the others——'

'I'll meet the others there,' Palfrey said. 'This is my job, if ever there was one.'

Yet as he made his way, in the third taxi which offered, he wondered if he were right. Many of the agents of Z5 said that he was wrong to take personal chances; that his function was to sit and watch and use them, as if he were using puppets. They said that if they lost Palfrey, it would be a death blow to Z5—and he did not believe them. No man, he argued, was indispensable; it was vanity to suppose otherwise.

He set out, therefore, with determination and slight defiance to the garage at the corner of the Rue Berthe.

He had checked, at the desk, that the street was in Montmartre, at the foot of the hill which overlooked Paris, where the Church of the Sacred Heart ministered to the thousands of sightseers who flocked to it in candlelit piety. He had arranged for the porter to telephone two people to meet him at the corner of the street, and had little doubt that they would be there.

His taxi was a new Renault.

He had studied the map of the *arroudissement,* and was put down near a Metro station, paid his driver off, and stood for a few seconds, looking at the lighted cafés.

Palfrey walked towards the corner where he saw an illuminated garage sign.

He had not expected it to be as public as this.

On further inspection, he saw that the garage extended to another street, narrow and ill-lit. Palfrey saw the wide doors open, a petrol pump just inside, and several old cars parked. It was dimly lighted, and there was no sign of movement. A brighter light shone from an uncurtained window above the garage, and there was a shadow at the window; as if someone were standing at the side and looking out. He walked slowly towards the entrance; but no one hailed him, and when he looked in, he saw no one.

He went back to the Rue Berthe.

Two doors along was a *bistro,* where several men and two girls were drinking beer. The girls looked young and impudent, with that indefinable air of worldliness which sits easily upon Parisiennes. The men were working-class type; it would be easy to think in sinister terms and imagine them to be members of a criminal gang.

No one showed any interest in the garage.

Palfrey strolled to the other side of the road, and knew that many eyes were turned towards him.

A taxi drew up, not far along, and a man stepped out. He was Georges Garon, small, saturnine, a man famous for his work in the Resistance, and Dubonnet's most reliable *aide.*

They reached the corner together, from opposite directions. Palfrey stopped, first.

'Is Jules coming?'

'He will be here,' Garon said. The café light shone on his thin moustache and bright eyes; he had narrow shoulders and was neatly dressed in a dark suit. 'What is the trouble, please?'

'Marcel was attacked, in this garage I think.'

27

'So.' Garon made no comment. He gave Palfrey the impression that he questioned the wisdom of them meeting here. He turned and led the way into the *bistro*, and ordered two beers. 'We will wait, yes?'

Palfrey fought back his impatience.

'Yes.'

They could see the road from the window where they sat, and had half finished their drinks when the third man came along; Jules Santot. He was walking briskly; presumably he had paid off his taxi or left his car further away. He glanced into the *bistro* as the others finished their beer and went to join them.

Palfrey said: 'One of you at the corner, the other with me.'

He could have gone alone, earlier; or saved precious minutes after Garon had arrived. But he set a limit to recklessness.

Santot, tall, willowy, who looked as if he would be at home in the arty backwaters of Paris, fingered his bow tie, and waited at the corner; the least likely to attract attention. But others were watching, including a gendarme, who had retraced his steps and seemed to be swinging his truncheon with more vigour than before.

The couple reached the yawning garage entrance.

'I don't know what I expect to find,' Palfrey said. 'Marcel might have telephoned from here, or might have slipped out to a telephone. Are there any nearby, do you know?'

'At the Metro.' Garon jerked his head.

'It would be too public.'

'A *bistro* or a café, then.'

'I doubt it.'

Palfrey stepped into the smelly garage, while Garon looked at the wall, found electric light switches, and pressed several down, flicking them all together with the palm of his hand. Bright light glared down from unshaded lamps. The cars, all taxis, looked dilapidated, hardly fit to be on the road.

One of them had one brown wing, and three black.

At the rear of the garage was a long bench and a service well. Tools littered the bench. There was a small lathe, with iron filings glinting in the light. At one side a door probably led to a flight of stairs and the flat above the garage. A few brightly polished pieces of metal lay on the bench, unfamiliar and strange-looking. Near them was a small model of a curious design, something like a rocket shell. He fingered it, then turned away.

In one corner was a candlestick telephone, on a small shelf, with a filthy telephone directory hanging from a nail by means of a piece of rubbered electric cable. Palfrey stood to one side, and studied the floor by the telephone. It was black and there were patches of grease on the concrete. He went down cautiously, without touching it with his knees, and peered more closely.

'It's been washed,' he said.

Garon bent down, as Palfrey steadied the light.

Something showed up, a reddish colour.

'I do not like it,' Garon said. 'This was the telephone, and here——'

'I knew he was hurt.'

Garon looked at the door.

'I will go up,' he announced.

Palfrey smiled. 'Soon,' he said. 'Stay here, will you, and watch that service well.' He went to the door, with his right hand at his pocket; the cold steel of the gun was comforting. The door creaked when he opened it, and a light shone on worn wooden stairs. A piece of thick rope was fastened to one side, as a handrail.

It was useless to creep up; every tread made a noise which could be heard above. So he walked firmly, keeping his right hand in his pocket. At the top was a narrow landing, with two doors opening from it. One was ajar, and there was darkness beyond; at the top and sides of the other a light showed. It was just possible that he had not been heard. He slipped into an unlighted room on the right and pressed down the switch. It was an empty bedroom; a cheap alarm clock stood on a chest of drawers, ticking loudly.

There was no sound from the other room.

Palfrey left this light on, went to the second door, and thrust it open.

A boy was sitting back in an old armchair, with a *Roman policier* in his hands, the cover partly hiding his face. He looked up, then dropped the book and sprang to his feet. He couldn't have been more than eleven or twelve, a dirty-looking

29

lad with a smear of grease over one cheek.

Palfrey said: 'Good evening,' and glanced round the small, over-crowded living room.

'What-is-it-you-want?' The words popped out of the boy's mouth.

'Are you alone?' asked Palfrey.

'Yes, sir. My father is out. My mother is also out. If it is a taxi you require, I can assist you.'

'Ah, a taxi,' said Palfrey. 'No, thanks.' He went across the room with one if those swift movements which could startle even Drusilla, and reached a closed door. The boy gaped at him. He pushed the door open and found himself in a small kitchen-scullery, facing another closed door. He opened it. The warm air of the night crept into the room, partially dispelling the stuffiness, the smell of stale cooking. Palfrey found himself looking down at a flight of wooden steps leading to an alley which appeared to run alongside the back of the garage. Uneven roofs stretched out in front of him, showing palely beneath the stars.

He turned back. The boy had followed him, open-mouthed.

'How long have you been here?'

'For a long time, sir—two hours.'

'When did your mother and father go out?'

'My mother . . .' he shrugged expressively. 'I haven't seen her tonight. My father was in for a little while. Please tell me, what do you want? If it is a taxi . . .'

'No, thanks,' said Palfrey.

The boy might be lying; might be acting; and might be telling the simple truth.

'Has a taxi left here, in the past hour?'

'Several, sir. They come and go. My father owns them all.'

'All?'

'Every one, sir.'

'I see,' said Palfrey 'You have a photograph of your father, perhaps?'

'Oh yes.' The boy turned to the mantelshelf and pointed with a grubby finger.

The photograph in the cheap frame was of the man who had driven the taxi which had nearly run Palfrey down.

Palfrey reached the hotel a little more than an hour later, and found Drusilla still in the dining room. As he threaded his way between the tables, he could see the relief in her expression. He smiled and sat down, ordering briskly.

'Well?' asked Drusilla.

'A start, no more,' said Palfrey. 'He was attacked when at the telephone in the garage, there's no doubt of that. The owner of the garage was my taxi driver this afternoon, and the cab is still there; for a good reason.' He smiled faintly. 'Dubonnet had removed and smashed the distributor and slashed the tyres, to make sure they couldn't get it out in a hurry. The owner is missing.'

'And Marcel?' Drusilla caught her breath.

'No trace. No body. Yet.'

'Oh, Sap,' she said, and leaned forward and touched his hand. 'So you're right.'

'There's murk and mystery all right,' Palfrey said. 'And we're only at the beginning of it. The Devil today is the Devil of yesterday, I'm afraid. Kidnapping of children allied to a keen desire not to have Z5 involved!'

The waiter bought a *pâté* and toast, a bottle of red Burgundy, and went off.

'If you hadn't noticed that taxi swerve, they'd have still been safe.'

'Oh, yes. But when they knew that there was a search for that particular taxi, they panicked. The police say that the garage owner is believed to be honest, or rather, not suspected, so far, of anything that rates as crime. He lets his cabs out on hire to licensed drivers, and there have been some pretty unsavoury ones recently, but the owner himself drove my cab. They're hunting for him, of course. His wife——' he shrugged. 'She has a poor reputation in those parts, and is seldom likely to be found with her husband. The boy——'

'Boy?'

'I forgot to tell you, a small boy was in charge,' said Palfrey. He paused. 'It could be very ugly indeed.'

'What *are* you thinking?' Drusilla asked.

'If it can be called thinking,' Palfrey went on. 'I'm reminding myself that when there was once a threat to young Alexander, you and I would have done practically anything in the world to get him out of danger. Remember? I've never been tempted to betrayal before, but I was then. The quickest way to a parent's heart is through the children.' He gave a harsh, angry laugh. 'The quickest way to make the parents do what you want. Soon, Prince Frederick of the Netherlands and the Duke of Nordia will be presented with certain demands, I think. So will Juanita. The question is, which one shall I tackle personally? Coming?'

Drusilla said: 'Were you serious when you asked me to try again with Señora Melano?'

'Half serious, my sweet,' said Palfrey slowly. 'There's no need, we can put someone else on to her. You'd rather get back home, wouldn't you?'

She didn't answer at first; he knew the struggle going on in her mind—or between her heart and mind. She had introduced him to Z5, knew most of its workings, knew the importance of its success and sensed, as he sensed, the possibility of real danger in this situation. She knew that she could help; that a woman was more likely to discover the real Juanita Melano; and she wanted to go back to England.

'I'll try with the Señora,' she said at last. 'You'd better go to Stockholm. There were more people involved there, you'll have more to work on.'

The waiter came up again; he coughed twice, to make his presence known.

5

The Man from Moscow

THE evening sun gleamed over the red, onion-shaped domes of the buildings of the Kremlin; warmed the pavement of the Red Square; cheered the people who thronged it, many of them gazing with the glazed expression of sightseers at the great gates, the armed guards, the walls which hid power and mystery.

An old woman crossed herself. No one noticed the movement, which was almost furtive.

A powerful English limousine purred into the Red Square turned towards the gates and slowed down; but the guards waved it on, and it disappeared from the public gaze.

Inside, sat a magnificent giant.

He was in uniform, and bemedalled, for earlier he had attended an official ceremony, at which some of the greatest in the land had been present. His hat was on his knees, and his thick dark brown hair was stirred by the wind which came through the open window. It was the only thing about him that moved.

He was strikingly handsome, with a broad, unwrinkled forehead, and clear brown eyes. His cheekbones were high, and there was a hint of the Mongol about the upper part of his face, but no more than a hint.

He moved at last, unbuttoned a pocket in his tunic, and took out a folded piece of paper; a cablegram. He glanced down at it, smiling. It was a smile of great repose, serene and even saintly. Some believed in this saintliness, others, that it was a veneer behind which lurked a devil.

The car pulled up at a large building. The guard at the door saluted, and did not ask to see his pass. He went in, and the chauffeur waited for him.

And now his full proportions could be seen, for he towered above men, even the guards who were chosen for their height. Eagerly they made way for him, for he was one of the heroes of the Soviet Union; a hero who had remained in favour for many years; a man about whom much gossip revolved, but who seemed impervious to gossip.

Another opened the door. He found himself in a small ante-room, facing a long-nosed man, not unlike a ferret.

'Greetings, Comrade!'

'Greetings. You received my message?'

'Yes, Comrade, you are expected.'

'Good.' The giant smiled again, and the saintliness was in remarkable contrast to the furtiveness of the little man, whom he had greeted.

The giant sat down and stretched out his long legs. Minutes passed, neither slowly nor quickly for him, who had the inexhaustible patience of the Slav. He had remarkably quick ears, too, for he heard the faint sound of a door opening.

'They will see you now, Comrade.'

The giant entered a large room, dominated and overpowered by an enormous portrait of Stalin.

Three men sat at a table. They wore plain tunics, with high collars, and their only difference appeared to be in the central man who was completely bald.

The giant saluted.

'You may sit down, Comrade Andromovitch.'

'Thank you.'

'You have a request to make, Andromovitch?'

'With your permission. I wish to receive my papers to leave the country on a mission of indefinite length.'

'I see, I see,' said the bald-headed man. His grey eyes were hooded, the lids wrinkled. 'You understand, Andromovitch, that you are one of few trusted by the Supreme Soviet to undertake such missions?'

'Fully,' said Andromovitch.

The bald man said testily: 'It is necessary, yes, for us to participate in this . . .' he paused, to add with distaste . . .

34

'Z5. Yes. And it has served us well.'

'It has served all nations well, Comrade.'

'Yes, yes.' The hooded eyes were frosty. 'What is the purpose, this time?'

'I have received this cablegram from Dr. Palfrey.' Andromovitch held it out.

'Yes, yes, naturally I have seen it. But this message—do you know why it has been sent?'

' I think so,' said Andromovitch. 'It refers me to the French newspaper *Ce Soir* of a certain date. In it are reports of the disappearance of two children, the son of Prince Frederick of the Netherlands and the daughter of the Duke of Nordia. They are still missing.'

'This is so? You are sure?'

'Yes, Comrade, and it is evident that Palfrey has reason to think that it will interest Z5. And as evident to me, that it will interest us.' He glanced up at the portrait.

'Yes, yes. So it is happening elsewhere, not only . . .' He broke off. 'Wait, I will get further instructions.'

He jumped up and darted out of the room. Returning with some pomposity, he turned to Andromovitch.

'You have permission to leave tonight, Andromovitch, your papers will be delivered later. You will fly to Stockholm direct, make contact with Palfrey as quickly as possible, and report as often as you can. You understand?'

'Fully, Comrade.'

'You may go. You have little time, Andromovitch.'

Moonlight shone over the still waters of Stockholm, even the harshness of the bright lights failed to spoil the beauty of the waterfront, or the whine of traffic still the lapping of the water against the shore.

A taxi turned past the Opera House, and Andromovitch, sitting at the back, saw the glitter of the International Variety theatre, and the gaily-coloured lamps of the big restaurant near it. The car swung round, towards Sturplan, slowed down, and stopped before the huge mushroom shelter in the centre of the square.

Andromovitch, dismissing the taxi, glanced right and left, allowed two cars to pass, then stepped across the road.

35

Palfrey moved forward from the shadows.

The Russian's smile of greeting stilled on his lips.

Palfry stepped past without a glance.

Andromovitch's height enabled him to see over the tops of the cars and the heads of passers by. He saw another man slip across the road and follow Palfrey.

There was now no doubt that Palfrey was being shadowed. In this narrower street there were few lighted signs, and long stretches of darkness. At every unlit patch, the man immediately behind Palfrey drew nearer. He moved with stealthy silence, and Palfrey showed no sign that he knew he was being followed.

He turned right, the man at his heels.

When Andromovitch reached the corner, he could see only shadowy figures, but the footsteps rang out clearly. He increased the length of his stride. Palfrey walked on until he came to the foot of some stone steps, with electric lamps jutting out from the walls. He hurried up these, the man behind still following. It was too bright here for any attack to develop. But Palfrey's shadower drew nearer, was within two yards of him.

Palfrey turned right, into another narrow street of shops.

Andromovitch turned the corner in time to hear a gasp and a thud. Palfrey was on his toes and leaning forward, and the man who had followed him was reeling back against the wall. Recovering swiftly, his right hand flashed to his side. A knife glinted.

Andromovitch put out one long arm and clapped the man on the shoulder; it must have felt as if a house had fallen on him. The man sagged to one side, and the knife dropped to the pavement.

'Now what shall we do with him, Sap?' Andromovitch asked easily, in excellent English.

'Think you can carry him?'

Andromovitch shrugged, shifted his grip, placing his fingers at the back of the man's neck. There was a little grunting sound, and the man fell slack; unconscious.

'You haven't forgotten your tricks,' Palfrey said. 'This way.'

Andromovitch lifted the man easily, and without effort.

Palfrey stopped at a narrow shop with a small window and slipped a key into the lock.

The Russian had to lower his head, then stood upright as Palfrey closed the door. There was a smell of leather and of oil. Palfrey did not switch on a light, for the shop was illuminated by the beam of a lamp nearby, but stepped to the back of the shop and opened another door. This led to a small windowless sitting-room. As Andromovitch dropped his prisoner into one of the easy chairs, Palfrey switched on the light.

It was bright and clear.

The unconscious man lay limp, almost lifeless.

Over his head Palfrey looked up into the Russian's eyes.

'Well, well! Hallo, Stefan!'

Deliberately, they shook hands; and the grip lasted longer than was customary. Then Palfrey moved back, and let his gaze roam over his friend's figure and face. He was smiling with a touch of the warm affection few, other than Drusilla, saw.

'Wonderful! You've had a holiday.'

'A little one, in the Crimea,' said Andromovitch. 'And you, my friend . . . always the same, always exactly the same, in ways and in looks. Good!' He chuckled. 'And we are to be busy, it seems.'

'Well, we've made a start,' said Palfrey. 'I wondered if they would let you come. Last time, they wished another man on to me. Nice chap, but . . .'

'He is reliable enough, or I would have found a way to tell you not to use him,' said Andromovitch. 'Sap, I know how difficult it is, this distrust—and, knowing the reasons for it, can say nothing of what I really think, except—this. There is no mistrust, in Moscow, of Dr. Palfrey or Z5. I do not think that is true of anyone or anything else.'

Palfrey's eyes lit with pleasure. 'Let's sit down.' He glanced at the unconscious man. 'We might get something out of him when he wakes up, but that won't be for a while. It's good to see you. Though "good" is too mild a word. Drusilla said that if Stefan were able to come, she'd be a happier woman.'

'And Drusilla is well?'

'Blooming! The others, too, and——' Palfrey laughed.

'But we can go into all of that later. You read the *Ce Soir*. You saw what I was getting at?'

Andromovitch sat back and crossed his long legs.

'Yes, Sap. So did my masters. You see, two children of highly placed members of the Politburo have disappeared, in the past three weeks. Two. They were already worried, and now——'

'Well, well!' breathed Palfrey. His eyes sparkled. 'So now we know it's a job for us, and big. Similar methods to those used in the past, with different subjects. Use the children to weaken the resistance of the parents. Had you discovered anything to help?'

'Nothing. It was being dealt with by the Security Police. It was not regarded as being work for me until your cable arrived. But then, a complete change over. So that's all I know. And you?'

'Nothing more,' said Palfrey. 'Odds and ends only, and earlier proof that it's dangerous. Marcel Dubonnet was attacked two nights ago, and we haven't found him yet.' He paused, and studied the frown which brought a vertical line between the Russian's eyes. 'Bad, yes. And this chap followed me from the Bromma Airport, here. He'd obviously been told to meet me at Stockholm. He was still with me at the Nybroplan, and shadowed me to the mushroom. Sorry if I startled you there.'

The man in the chair stirred, his lips moved, and his eyes began to flicker.

6

The House on the Island

PALFREY looked away from the prisoner.

'I was lucky to be able to use this place.'

'Yes. It is one of ours?'

'Yes and no. A friend of Sven's owns it, we were able to use it for tonight. The door there is soundproof, to make sure that no noises from the workshop reach the customers, and there's no back entrance, no window in this room. So sounds won't travel.'

He glanced at the man again, and saw his eyes opening.

'Now that is wonderful!' said Andromovitch.

'Just right,' agreed Palfrey. 'It doesn't matter how much he squeals, we can go on talking to him . . . and if he gets hurt——' He shrugged.

'I do not care for men who use knives against my friends,' said Andromovitch. 'Sap, a little while ago it was necessary to make a man talk. A knife was used . . . long, and thin. Something like this.' He took a pocket-knife out and opened one blade; much longer than that on an ordinary pocket-knife. He rested his thumb on the keen blade. 'That man, I tell you, he was tough. The right word, yes . . . tough?'

'Tough,' said Palfrey warmly.

'I would not have thought that a man could stand such torture and pain,' said Stefan.

The man in the chair muttered, and they turned to him as if startled. He sat upright. His lips were parted, and his light blue eyes showed terror.

'Why, he's come round,' said Palfrey, as if astounded.

'Then need we wait, my friend?' Andromovitch touched the blade of the knife.

'No reason why, the quicker we get results the better,' said Palfrey. 'Better tie him up first.' He got up, slowly.

The prisoner cringed back as Andromovitch rose, a monster whose head touched the ceiling and whose face was set in frightening lines. Palfrey touched the prisoner's right hand, and it was snatched away.

'No!' he gasped.

'Good lord!' exclaimed Palfrey. 'He's scared already. He must have heard——'

Andromovitch chuckled.

'Hearing is not like feeling, Sap. And remember he did not consider your feelings when he took out his knife. Besides, the quick way to the truth is the hard way.' He stretched out his hands, gripped the man tightly, and raised him from the chair. Palfrey fetched some leather bootlaces from the display cabinet and tied two together, watched all the time by the man with the terrified eyes. Then he bent down and tied the man's right ankle to the leg of the chair. He did the same with the left.

'We'll want one arm free, shan't we?' he asked. 'I can hold it.'

'His right hand,' Andromovitch said. 'Later, he will need to use his right hand, perhaps to stick knives into men's backs. It would be better if he hadn't the full use of that hand. There are two places where the tendons can be severed, and . . .'

'*No!*' cried the prisoner, and sweat stood out in beads on his forehead and on his upper lip. 'I tell you all, I tell you!'

'We've heard that story before,' said Palfrey.

'I tell you all—everything I know. Everything!' He sobbed the words. 'It was not I, it was the woman, she told me . . .' He broke off, his teeth chattering, and began to shiver.

Palfrey said: 'Well, let's hear what he has to say.'

The man began to talk, watching Stefan and the knife in his hand.

An hour later, Palfrey sat in the brightly lit office of the Chief of Police, smiling vaguely across at that official, a tall, handsome man of middle age.

40

'I understand you,' said the Chief of Police gravely. 'Yes, and I have also received the authorisation to assist in every way I can. But this——' he shrugged. 'Can I be necessary?'

'Vital,' said Palfrey.

'To be attacked in the street is an event that can happen in all big cities. This man Neilssen—we have no knowledge of him, but he is a bad one, we can see that. But to say that he received his instructions from a dwarf, and while at the house on Hilsa Island, and that while there he saw this fascinatingly beautiful woman—how can that be believed?'

Palfrey murmured: 'He was frightened. My friend is a big chap, you know.'

The blue eyes were shadowed, as if with doubt.

'This dwarf and the woman, according to Neilssen, live in one of the summer houses on Hilsa. Yes, yes, I know the island, there are perhaps three or four houses there, all of them as this man described, large, white, and overlooking the lake.'

'And with a red chalk mark on one wall, so that he could identify it again, remember,' said Palfrey. 'Neilssen was quite clear. He was summoned to a shop from which he was taken, after dark, to this island. It's one of hundreds, and he recognised it because he was wrecked off it a few years ago. The dwarf paid him half of the money promised for following me, told him he would get the rest if he reported a dead Palfrey, and that he would be met at the mushroom shelter by a messenger, tomorrow. But he didn't trust the dwarf or the lovely lady, and marked the wall of the house. Very sensible of him. Will it be such a big job, to surround that house? And to have the private jetties watched, to make sure no one can get away in a motor-boat?'

'It will need twenty of my men.'

'Well, yes, but surely worth it,' said Palfrey, 'and it should only be for a few hours. I know, it's trying, but—orders are orders.'

He beamed.

'I will arrange it,' said the Chief of Police, abruptly. 'I will send the men to Nybroviken quay, and the motor vessel——'

'Oh, please, no,' said Palfrey apologetically. 'That's so public. If we could sneak away quietly, not using motor-boats, and approach the island by stealth, I think it would be better. Could we leave from the Klara Canal?'

'I will send a man with you,' said the Chief of Police stiffly. 'You will wait at the canal with him, and the others will follow. It will take a little time. And am I to understand, Dr. Palfrey, that you wish to break into this house yourself, with your friend? We are to wait outside?'

'Until we shout for help,' said Palfrey, 'I know it's shockingly unorthodox. Scotland Yard hates it when it has to connive at anything like this, and only does so under the strictest orders from our Home Secretary. Most exceptional case, you know—spies. We can't afford to take risks.'

'I have my authority,' growled the Chief of Police.

Palfrey and Andromovitch sat on the bank of the Klara Canal, with the leafy branches of the clustered trees above them, and the water rippling gently near their feet, eating out of paper bags. Hundreds of small craft were moored on either side of the canal, moving and creaking gently. The policeman who had accompanied them stood stiffly to attention, some way off.

'Awkward things, these Scandinavian sandwiches,' Palfrey murmured. 'Hardly a sandwich in the dictionary definition of the word. Only one layer of bread. But decidedly good. Feeling better? Have another of these egg ones.'

'I do not, as yet, feel ill,' said Andromovitch, helping himself to a large savoury.

'Let us hope you feel the same way in five minutes,' said Palfrey, eyeing the Russian's enormous bites with some awe. 'Any luck, and Neilssen's lady boss will be literally caught napping. Remarkably efficient, these Swedes. The Chief didn't like the idea, but orders are orders and he'll do it well. Odd story. According to Neilssen, he has done a few shadowing jobs for the same crowd before, presumably led by the lady whose name he doesn't know, always on instructions from a third party whom he never sees again. But this particular job was regarded as being important enough to require personal instruction from headquarters. He was made to wear goggles, which he slipped. He must know the archipelago well, to be sure it was Hilsa Island. Could we have been taken in?'

42

'I think not. The man was too terrified to invent anything.'
'We'll hope so. Quite a woman, if he's right—she dazzled him by her beauty. Dark, too. I know a lovely who is dazzling and dark, but I don't quite see how she could fit in. I haven't told you what's been happening in the south, have I? You haven't heard about Señora Melano?'
'No.'
Palfrey said: 'It's time you did.' He had the gift of swift and vivid phrases, and of making his points briefly. There was little of the Paris affair that Stefan Andromovitch did not know when Palfrey had finished.

'The lady could have flown from Paris,' Andromovitch remarked.

'Oh, yes. But Drusilla is supposed to be looking after her. Drusilla would have had a message for me at Bromma Airport, if she had disappeared. Besides, I'm having them both watched. I hope we aren't going to have too many dazzling beauties, they're distracting. Mind you, the chap didn't notice her eyes. It's hard to imagine anyone not noticing Juanita's eyes. Ask Drusilla!'

Stefan smiled; in the moonlight, his face was shadowy on one side and silvered on the other; it added to the statuesque effect. He was, as always, completely relaxed. It was a thing Palfrey had noticed about him from the day of their first meeting, when Great Britain and the Soviet had been allies, and they had worked together under the Marquis of Brett. He had doubted Brett's judgment of the Russian, then, but had since learned that no judgment had ever been more sound.

He trusted Stefan Andromovitch as far as he would trust any man; in some ways, further than he would trust himself. Any Russian who could keep the confidence of both the Politburo and the Western powers in the prevailing conditions, and at no time and in no way betray either, was a remarkable man.

Over the years, a casual friendship had grown into something deeper and more lasting. On occasions like these, it was almost like working with an incarnation of oneself.

Men's footsteps trampled through the quiet, and grey clad figures broke through the trees. Among them was the Chief of Police.

They set sail in five small craft, creeping along the canal and then out into the great lake. Clouds were blowing sluggishly across the sky, darkening the moon's light; it was exactly what they wanted. The distant stars were bright. Near at hand, the dim shapes of moored craft gave a sense of company. The boats moved swiftly in the quickening breeze. Palfrey sat in one, and Stefan in the other; because of Stefan's size, there was a policeman less in his small sailing craft. They made little sound, just the persistent and unfailing lap, and the occasional note of wind rustling in the sails. As they went further out, the lights grew dimmer and near-darkness closed about them.

They passed a small, rock island, and then began to weave among the narrow inlets. Palfrey was quite lost, but the pilot of the leading craft went on, deft and sure, as if he were at the wheel of a car along a well-known thoroughfare.

They reached a wider channel of water, and ahead of them sighted an island, larger than most, but more hilly.

A man by Palfrey murmured: 'That is Hilsa.'

There was no light visible on Hilsa, but as they drew near, the clouds drifted from the moon. Here and there a house, built in the side of the hill, showed up white; sometimes the moon shone upon a large glass window, as if it were a blind eye, searching vainly for them. There were many inlets, and they passed several before they came to a narrow fissure which seemed to carve the island in two. They turned into it, one graceful craft after another. The sails were lowered and men took the oars. Soon they came within sight of a jetty. The first boat stopped, bumping gently against the wood; soon the others were alongside.

The Chief of Police whispered: 'It is near here. Neilssen took the oars. Soon they came within sight of a jetty. The

'Shall we check the red chalk mark?' asked Palfrey.

'I shall come with you.' The Chief of Police led the way ashore, across a patch of grass, and then to a flight of steps which were cut in the side of the hill. He went up quietly, followed by Palfrey, Andromovitch and two of his men. The steps zig-zagged right and then left, sometimes steep and at others shallow, and seemed never-ending.

44

They reached a flat stretch at last, all too short of breath for speed.

One more shallow flight, and they were on the terrace of a house. It stood in stately silence, silvered by the moon, surrounded by gardens and lawns.

The Chief of Police moved swiftly to the white wall.

Palfrey drew up beside him. 'Yes?'

A broad forefinger pointed to a smear of red.

'Good for Neilssen,' said Palfrey.

'But not, perhaps, good for Dr. Palfrey. You understand that if we wait at the bottom, we shall not be able to hasten to your help?' The precise voice held a note of satisfaction.

'Oh, yes,' said Palfrey. 'But that's not quite the idea. We'll manage—and if they beat us, all we want you to do is to make sure they don't get away. Er—am I making it clear? For instance, supposing we go in and have a chat. We may want to leave, without the lady knowing you're about.'

'We will wait below,' said the Chief of Police resignedly. 'There are three ways down—we shall cover the bottom of each flight of steps. If you need us, you will use this, please.' He thrust a whistle into Palfrey's hand, bright and shining.

'You're very good,' said Palfrey.

The Chief of Police and his man went off, making little sound, and soon disappeared down the steps. Palfrey and Andromovitch stood in the silence, looking at the house. It was not large, by English standards, but cleverly built, its wide windows giving an illusion of space.

'I'd hate to break one of those windows,' Palfrey said. 'Must cost a fortune.'

'We shall try the door,' said Andromovitch, 'but first we will walk right round the house.'

At the back, the lower floor was almost certainly in semi-darkness by day, for the hillside had been excavated to give a level foundation. The entrance was reached by a flight of stone steps which seemed to lead into the bowels of the earth.

'Perhaps this is best,' Andromovitch said. He started down the steps, and reaching the back door, shone a torch on it, examining the lock. His great hands moved with surprising dexterity, and Palfrey heard the sound of metal scraping lightly on metal.

45

The lock turned.

'Now, if it is not bolted, we shall soon be inside.'

The door opened.

They switched on a light in this earth-bound room, and found that it was a wood shed, packed with logs. In another, next to it, there was a small bench littered with oddments which suggested that someone had been experimenting with radio and electrical parts. A model caught Palfrey's eye; it was identical in shape with a smaller one he had seen at the garage in Paris.

'We should hurry,' Stefan said.

'Ah!'

They stepped swiftly through to a doorway which led to a flight of stairs and the main part of the house.

It came up into a spacious, tiled kitchen. From there they passed to a hall, the moonlight shining through a narrow window. A wide staircase was on one side, and there were several arched doorways; two of the doors were open. They glanced into the big rooms, furnished, as far as they could see, with luxury and good taste.

'All nicely tucked up in bed, I hope,' said Palfrey.

They started up the stairs, Andromovitch leading. As they reached the landing, they heard a small, indeterminate sound.

Andromovitch stopped.

They could just make out the shape of four doors against the white background of the walls, but could not tell whether one was open or not. The end of a wide passage was swallowed up in darkness behind them. As they waited, they heard the sound again.

Both men took out their guns.

They moved forward slowly, side by side, but all sound had ceased. They hesitated, and at that moment the silence was violently shattered by a shrill, discordant scream.

7

The Midget

ANDROMOVITCH leapt forward, reached the door as the scream ended and began again, a wild, terror-stricken cry. Inside the room there was a heavy crash. Andromovitch turned the handle of the door and pushed, but it was locked. He drew back, put his shoulder to the top panels, and exerted all his strength; Palfrey watched, imagining the power in that effort, trying to see both ways in case another door opened.

The scream came a third time, wild, frightening.

The door crashed in.

Across the room, between the wall and a divan bed, was a girl. She stood with her arms stretched out behind her, pressing against the wall and staring at the creature who was at the foot of the bed. This creature was approaching her, knife in hand. As the door crashed in, he drew back his hand to throw the knife.

Palfrey saw Andromovitch fire. The man—was it a man?— screamed out as the bullet struck his arm, and turned to face the giant Russian.

With one bound he had passed him and reached the open window. From there he leapt to the sill, and with an almost inhuman dexterity hurled himself outwards.

The whole series of movements, their horrible implication, was over in a flash.

The girl turned and flung herself downwards on the bed, while Palfrey closed the door and followed the Russian to the window.

It opened on to the lake, and there was a sheer drop to

rock, a hundred feet below. Lights were flashing from the torches of the searching police.

Andromovitch turned round slowly.

'Not good, Sap, and he knew what he was doing.'

'I wish we did,' said Palfrey, gloomily. He took a brandy flask from his hip pocket and went towards the girl, resting a hand gently on her shoulder. Andromovitch slipped quickly from the room, and Palfrey could hear the Russian opening doors. There was a pause, followed by a loud crack; a door being forced. Next, noises from outside told of the police hurrying up the steps.

The girl's crying quietened.

Palfrey patted her shoulder gently.

'It's all over, there's no more to worry about.'

She didn't move, and he had no idea whether she knew English; if she were an educated Swedish girl, she certainly would. He had only the picture of that terrified face, grotesquely illuminated by the bright light shining from the top of the lamp. That was still the only light in the room. There was a sound of knocking from downstairs, and Stefan called out:

'I will go and admit them.'

'You've nothing more to fear,' Palfrey told the girl. Self-possession was coming back to her. She sat up, and he handed her a woolly jacket which she slipped round her shoulders. Now, he could see that she was very young; twenty, perhaps. Her long fair hair fell loosely over her shoulders, untouched by pins or ribbon. Palfrey gave her a clean handkerchief, and went to the door.

Andromovitch and the Chief of Police were talking, but he could not hear what they said.

He turned back to the girl, his smile reassuring.

'Better?'

'Thank you, yes.'

'I'm glad we came in time.'

'Who—who are you?'

'Friends,' said Palfrey. 'We were looking for the woman who owns the house.'

'She has gone,' the girl said slowly. 'She left, early this evening. Only Erik was here.' She shuddered, and glanced

48

towards the window. Palfrey wondered whether she would ever forget the way the midget had jumped backwards, to his death. 'He—he was going to kill me.'

'Yes,' agreed Palfrey. 'Do you know why?'

'I didn't like him, he—frightend me. I didn't like being near him.'

'He wouldn't try to kill you, because of that.'

She didn't answer, but tears welled up in her eyes again, and she turned her face away.

The voices of the two men downstairs became louder; they were coming up. Palfrey went out on to the landing.

'That room, Sap.' Andromovitch pointed, the Chief of Police just behind him.

Palfrey saw that the lock had been broken on one of the doors. He stepped inside. A dim light shone on four small beds.

On each bed, slept a child.

Two boys and two girls. As far as he could judge, they were all about eleven or twelve years of age.

He recognised Prince Carel at once; the photograph in *Ce Soir* had been a good one.

Not one of the children stirred.

Palfrey stepped to the nearest, a girl, as the Chief of Police appeared in the doorway. Palfrey touched her eye, raising the lid gently. Peering close, he saw that the pupil was a pin-point, in indication that she had been drugged with morphia or a similar narcotic. He drew back, smiling faintly. But at heart, he did not feel like smiling; he felt the stirring of a horror which seemed to threaten them all, despite the peacefulness of this room and the apparent safety of the children.

The Chief of Police spoke in a hushed voice.

'The woman—she is not here?'

'She beat us to it,' said Palfrey, abruptly. 'Well, even so, someone is going to be grateful for the night's work. You'll be showered with congratulations.'

The Chief of Police said suavely: 'The credit is, of course, yours.'

'I hope you'll take it,' said Palfrey. 'In public, anyhow, I'd rather not have it put around that Stefan and I were on the scene. And to you we owe great promptness and co-operation.

49

Many would have caused too much delay.' He glanced round at the beds. 'I don't think you need worry over much, but have a doctor to look them over before they're taken away. Er—one little thing.'

'Anything.'

'You're very good. There's the girl in the other room, very much alive. I'd like it put around that she's dead. Do you think we can get away with it?'

The Chief of Police put a hand to his forehead, and then began to smile. Slowly the official gave way to the man. He slapped his thigh, laughed again, came striding across to Palfrey and put an arm round his shoulder.

'My friend, you are superb! Dead! Of course it cannot be done, it is impossible. But it will be done.' He chuckled again. 'Oh, it will be done, because I am beginning to understand that you do not want anything without a good reason. In the past I have thought, this Dr. Palfrey, this reckless adventurer, but now—Dr. Palfrey, I have one request to make myself.'

Overwhelmed, Palfrey gave an acquiescent murmur.

'You will spare me some time, we will have an evening together? I will not take a refusal, my good friend, I will not.'

'Nothing I'd like better,' Palfrey said warmly.

'Good! Now—if you will be so kind, will you tell me *why* you wish a live girl to be considered dead?'

Palfrey glanced at a hovering policeman.

'Of course I will—but not here. Downstairs. I'll just go and have a word with her.'

He slipped silently into the girl's room, leaving the Chief of Police still chuckling.

'Hallo,' said Palfrey. 'Much better, I see!'

She was sitting at the dressing-table, doing something to her hair. He strolled across to her.

'Are you, perhaps, a children's nurse? Or governess?'

'Why, yes! How did you guess?'

Palfrey smiled. 'It was fairly obvious. How long have you worked for—Madame?'

'For six months. I . . .' She broke off, and frowned.

'Why did you work for her?'

She said slowly: 'I have not always been happy here, there have been things I have not understood, but—it was a good post, and madame was generous, most generous.' Her English, with its faint accent, was straightforward and attractive. 'Do you think she will come back?'

'What makes you think she will not?'

'I heard her talking to Erik,' she said. 'It—alarmed me. She said that she might not return, it would depend on whether the police came here. Also, she said—I was not to be allowed to talk. The way she said that——' the girl shivered suddenly, violently. 'It frightened me. I could not sleep. I was locked in, there is no other house near—not near enough to hear me, and—the window.' Her lips worked. 'You know what lies beneath the window. I lay in bed, wide awake, so frightened—and then he came in. I shall never forget how he came in! He was creeping towards me when I put on the light, and his hands were stretched out. I can feel them!' She put her fingers to her throat, and stared into the mirror as if at a horror pictured there.

'It's all right now,' Palfrey murmured.

'Yes, yes, but—shall I ever forget? He leapt at me, and clutched my throat. I screamed and struck him, and he fell back. I jumped out of bed, but after that I couldn't move, he came towards me with the knife, how it glinted! I could feel it, as if it were in my flesh, I could feel it. And then—the giant came.'

'All over,' Palfrey said.

'I feel much better now, but . . .' she gave a strange little laugh. 'Already I begin to worry. Where shall I go?'

'Your family?' suggested Palfrey.

'I have no family,' she said simply. 'I am Norwegian. My parents were killed, being of the Resistance.'

'Friends?'

'Some good friends, yes—in Norway. I cannot go to them for help. I left them, so sure that I was lucky. A good wage, beautiful surroundings, and—but I am troubling you. I shall return to Norway and find work.'

'I can find work for you,' Palfrey said.

Her expression lightened, and she turned to look up at him; he wondered, now, if she were as old as he had first thought.

'You will?'

'If you'll help me.'

51

'Yes, yes, any way I can!'

'I want to send you to England, without telling any of your friends. You realise that Madame told Erik to kill you, if the police came. Don't you?'

'I suppose—yes. You are a policeman? An English police——'

'Call it that. I want Madame to think that Erik succeeded.'

She looked at him in astonishment. It was a long time before she answered. Then she stood up and turned to face him, her hands behind her back, like a small girl about to confess.

'Since I came here, I realised that it was something I did not understand,' she said. 'There were three children, and they were not well. Most of the time, they slept; and then, they became ill, terribly ill, with a fever, and a doctor I did not like came to see them. That lasted for a week, afterwards they recovered, but—they were not the same. They were taken away, and others came, and all was repeated. Four left this house, last week; and others have been brought to it.'

Palfrey said sharply: 'Have these four been ill?'

'No, they have slept a great deal, and I have even wondered if it is sickness, or whether they have been drugged. But I am a governess only, not a trained nurse. So I have not the knowledge.'

'How were the others different, after their illness?' Palfrey's voice was gentle but his eyes were hard; as if he was seeing a horror that was drawing nearer.

'They were—older.'

'Older?'

'Less—like happy children,' she said. 'Sullen—older. When I first saw them, I liked them, afterwards—they were hateful little beasts! That is all one could say, and I was glad that they left. Then more came, gay and happy, just children; and they changed, also, and it began to frighten me. Madame told me that it was because of the illness, a rare illness, and that I was doing good work in nursing them, but I could not be sure. I began to feel afraid. Now—you ask this of me. There is—wickedness.' It was a flat statement, not a question.

'And you can help to make an end to it,' Palfrey said.

After a while, she nodded. 'That I will do.'

'Good!' Palfrey gripped her arm. 'And the first thing I have to know is—who are you?'

'Elsa—Elsa Olsen. Please! Everything I have told you is true.'

'I know,' said Palfrey. 'And you can help to look after some English children, who are quite normal. Get dressed, Elsa.'

He left her, alone.

The landing was empty, but men were moving in and out of the rooms, searching. He doubted if they would find anything helpful; any clue to the identity of Madame, nor did he think there would be any further indication, here, of the horror which he sensed.

8

The Grateful Duke

SEVERAL men waited for the motor launch which took Palfrey, Andromovitch and Elsa Olsen from the island; and one of them, Sven Svenson, was Palfrey's chief agent in Sweden. Svenson took charge of Elsa, and drove off in a sleek car; she would stay in hiding during the day, and be smuggled out of the country next morning.

The Chief of Police was still supervising the search of the white house.

Another car waited for Palfrey and the Russian.

'What is next, Sap?' Andromovitch talked as if the affair on the island had been an accident, to take in his stride.

Palfrey smiled. 'Sleep. Have you booked anywhere?'

'No.'

'I took a small suite at the Castle Hotel,' said Palfrey. 'Nice little place—seclusion and comfort. We'll go straight there, I think, the Chief will do everything we've asked, we can take it easy. Time to think.'

'Not good thoughts,' said Andromovitch.

'Hellish.' Palfrey shrugged. 'We've had them for company before.'

The Castle Hotel, near the Opera House, was small and compact, and as brightly lit at nearly three o'clock in the morning as at any time during the evening. Two receptionists, who spoke excellent English, exerted themselves to be helpful; Dr. Palfrey could have anything he desired.

'Just sleep,' said Palfrey.

The suite contained two rooms and a small bathroom, and

had windows which overlooked a courtyard; there was little noise. There were divan beds; Stefan placed a chair at the foot of one, and rearranged the bedclothes so that he could stretch out his legs. They undressed in silence and turned in.

Palfrey stared at the ceiling, picturing four children in a drugged sleep.

Andromovitch said: 'For you, a father, it must be worse than for me. But we have made progress, Sap, and done one excellent thing. When I report to Krenko that the two children are safe, and will soon be sent back, I shall be in high favour!' He chuckled, in the darkness. 'From that point of view, it could hardly be better.'

'No. Could I be exaggerating what it might mean?'

'Perhaps, and yet I hardly think that is likely.' Andromovitch framed his words carefully. 'These other children were drugged, made ill, and became—changed. You say Elsa's words were "sullen and older", so—their character was changed. It can be done, of course.'

'It's being done. Why?'

Andromovitch said slowly: 'If you start with the children, you can make the adults do what you wish.'

Palfrey didn't answer.

After a while, he went to sleep.

They had rolls, butter and coffee in the suite, at half-past ten next morning, and when Andromovitch was trying to fit himself into the bath, Palfrey telephoned the Chief of Police.

'Ah, Palfrey! Did you sleep well, my friend?'

'Like a top. Those children?'

'The report is good. I am assured there is nothing the matter with them, they were drugged, yes—morphia. But it was not a large dose. Elsa told us that they had been asleep for nearly ten hours, and before that had been very sleepy most of the day. My doctor is of the opinion that from the time they reached the house, they were given small doses of the drug to make them sleepy.'

'Yes, it's probable,' said Palfrey. 'They hadn't started the real business, thank God.'

The Chief of Police did not speak.

Palfrey said: 'And no one knows that they've been found?'

55

'Not yet.'

'I'd like to break the news to the Grand Duke of Nordia,' Palfrey said. 'And after that, release it—Madame will be expecting news. Have you arranged the rest?'

'Yes, my friend—as I told you, the impossible is quite possible, after all! There was a young girl killed, yesterday, in a road crash. An orphan, without kith or kin. Her body was taken to Hilsa Island, and will be brought ashore today. The ambulance will be waiting for her, and for the midget's body. And the world and this woman will think they were found dead on the island.'

'Well, that's one good thing.'

'You seriously believe that she was to be killed, because she could identify the other woman?'

'Yes,' said Palfrey.

The summer residence of the Grand Duke of Nordia was on one of the larger islands of the archipelago. Palfrey stepped out of the launch in which he had been brought from the mainland, and walked along the wooden jetty. The two police officers with him stayed in the launch.

Rocky land rose in front of him, with steps cut into it, but they were not so steep as those at Hilsa, and there were nothing like so many. Palfrey reached the top, finding himself on another terrace.

A young man stood at the open front door. He was tall, like most Swedes, fair-haired, clean-cut; not a handsome man, but with a fresh wholesomeness which made him look attractive.

'Dr. Palfrey?'

'Yes.'

'My father is waiting eagerly to see you. Is there news of my sister?'

'There is, indeed.'

'*Good news*?' The question burst out.

Palfrey smiled. 'Excellent news.'

The young man turned and rushed towards the house, dis-appearing before Palfrey reached the door. There was a mutter of excited conversation, and then he returned with an older man, bearded, rugged of feature, carrying an indefinable air of authority. He reached Palfrey in three strides.

'It is true? Astrid is safe?'

'Quite safe, Excellency, and in very good hands. The hands of the police.'

The youth drew level with Duke, both of them appearing to be overcome by emotion. Then the older man stretched out his hand, and drew Palfrey into a high, wide room, overlooking the lake.

'I must apologise for my son's excitement,' said the Grand Duke of Nordia, unexpectedly. 'We have been so desperately anxious, but he should not have left you standing there.'

Palfrey smiled.

'I can't imagine a better reason for running away.'

'You are kind, Dr. Palfrey, there is no service I will not do for you in return for this. To say I am—grateful.' He paused, and his eyes become misty. 'How can I prove my gratitude?'

'Oh, please!'

'I shall find a way,' said the Duke. 'Dr. Palfrey, one question which puzzles me. Why was I not informed by telephone?'

'My request,' said Palfrey promptly. 'You see, sir . . .' He looked at the younger man, and smiled. 'It's not quite so simple as it seems. May we have a chat together, for ten minutes?'

'Gustav!' That was a command, to go.

'Is there anything I can get you?' asked Gustav, eagerly. 'A drink, or——'

'A bit early for me, thanks,' said Palfrey.

Gustav went out.

'Please sit down,' said the Grand Duke, and waited until Palfrey was sitting before he sat down himself. 'I know, perhaps, a little about you—and my son also knows who you are and what you do. What made you interested in my daughter's disappearance?'

Palfrey stretched out his legs.

'Your child was one of several who have been kidnapped. Children of important people. At least one parent has been approached by the kidnappers, for a form of ransom. Not money, but information to which she had access. As you would have been.' The Grand Duke of Nordia sat upright,

57

frowning. He was a severe-looking man, now that he had recovered from the temporary break in his composure.

'Were you approached, Excellency?'

The Duke did not answer.

'After all,' said Palfrey, 'it's an effective way of getting information, isn't it? Most of us will do more for our youngsters than for anyone else. Had you been approached?'

The Duke said: 'Yes.'

'Ah. What did they want?'

'They did not say. I was told that if I wished to see my daughter again, I was to do exactly what I was told.'

'And what were you told to do?'

'I was to send my son, Gustav, to meet a man, who would be identified by his hat—a black hat, with a blue feather in the band.'

'Where and when were they to meet?'

'Tonight—on the steps of the Concert House.'

'And that's all?'

'I was not to tell the police.'

'You didn't tell them, did you?'

'I did not.'

Palfrey smiled. 'No need for them to know of this, I'd much rather it was kept quiet. You'd have sent your son, of course.'

'Certainly.'

'They didn't give you a hint about what they'd want?'

'No.'

'Did you guess?'

'Could guessing have helped?' asked the Duke.

'Sometimes it's all we have to work on,' said Palfrey. 'But facts are better. This governess——'

'If you wish to see her, I will send for her.'

'Not dismissed?'

'She has been an excellent servant, and I should not feel justified in dismissing her.'

'There is just one other thing——'

'Yes?'

'How did you receive this message? Did a man or a woman speak to you?'

'A woman telephoned,' said the Duke.

'You didn't recognise her voice?'

'I did not.'

'Pity,' said Palfrey. 'She's flown, and I'd give a lot to be able to put my hands on her. Was there anything distinctive about her voice? Did she speak in Swedish or English—French, perhaps?'

'She spoke in French,' said the Duke.

Palfrey groped in his pocket for cigarettes, and the Duke leaned forward with an open case before he could get his own out.

'Ah, thanks. French, eh?' He lit up. 'Do you know French well, Excellency?'

'Quite well,' said the Duke. 'I would not say that there was anything remarkable about the voice, it was—that of a cultured woman. It was—what is the word?—a warm voice, and quite natural. She did not speak as if she were threatening, more, indeed, as if she were—amused. If I could find her, then with my own hands I would——'

'Oh, no,' interrupted Palfrey. 'If you should ever find her, there are a lot of people who want to talk to her. I can't imagine her trying again with you, though. Someone else in Sweden, yes. There is something you can do for me, Excellency.'

'Anything.'

'If any of your friends should be in similar trouble, will you advise me, through the British Ambassador here?'

'Gladly.'

'One more request,' murmured Palfrey. 'Don't go into hospital to see your daughter, she is under temporary observation. She is *quite* well. The reason? We don't want word of the rescue reported for a few hours, and if you visited the place——'

'It is disappointing,' said the Duke, 'but if she is well——'

'Perfectly well, I assure you,' Palfrey was emphatic.

When he left the house, twenty minutes later, young Gustav was waiting for him at the foot of the steps. He looked strong and purposeful, and had a trick of stillness which reminded Palfrey of Stefan. He smiled restrainedly as Palfrey drew near the jetty, then moved forward suddenly. He glanced at the two members of the crew, and lowered his voice.

'Dr. Palfrey, I have a request to make.'

'Oh? Carry on.'

'I know about you—who doesn't?' Gustav gave a forced laugh. 'You must have many agents. Here and elsewhere. I would like to help find the woman who kidnapped my sister. Is that possible?'

Palfrey hesitated.

'There is nothing I would not do,' said Gustav earnestly. 'I am strong. I have served in the army, I am used to exertion. I can use weapons of all kinds, and—I am not a fool. I am to be trained for diplomacy, but—I have no feeling for it. I believe that I could be of use to you, Dr. Palfrey, and my father now owes you a great debt. If you were to have a word with him, then I think he would agree to allow me to serve you.'

'Ah,' said Palfrey. He did not smile into the ardent anxious young face. 'It might be possible, let me think about it.'

'You will?' Gustav's eyes blazed.

'Gladly.'

The young Swede wrung his hand.

Palfrey waved to him as the boat moved off, and Gustav stood on the jetty, watching; it was a long time before Palfrey lost sight of the enthusiasm in Gustav's expression. He looked up at the house, and saw the Duke standing on the terrace, a hand raised in farewell. He waved himself, and then sat back and closed his eyes, the noise of the engine, the lapping of the water, touching only the surface of his mind. Dreamily he heard an aeroplane droning overhead, and the sound of another oncoming engine.

Some slight, some tenuous, thread of warning touched him.

He opened his eyes, seeing the shimmering blue of the water and a motor-boat tearing alongside. Two men were standing in it, young fellows who were smiling happily as the wind of their own speed cut into their faces. They swerved dangerously near, and at that moment one of the men tossed something towards the launch—a small, dark ball, which curved gracefully and landed in the thwarts, two feet away from Palfrey.

9

Ducking

PALFREY cried: 'Jump!'

He sprang to his feet, stepped on to the side of the launch, shouted again as the crew swung round to stare at the metal thing lying there, then turned and dived into the lake. He felt the cold hug of the water, went under, and as he surfaced heard the roar, cracking, deafening.

A cloud of smoke hovered over his head, and the smell of cordite was strong. He coughed and took in a mouthful of water, gasped, then struck out. He could hear vague noises, a muffled kind of drumming in his ears.

He glanced round, with an effort.

The launch was afire, and already low in the water. He saw a man's head bobbing up and down, but only one. Palfrey set his teeth, and turned away, striking out with long, powerful strokes. He thought he heard a scream; and then another.

A second explosion, more deafening than the first, roared across the water. Smoke drifted low over the surface.

Palfrey turned away from it, and broke through the cloud into the calm and shimmering water beyond. Several craft, including two motor-boats, were bearing down on him; two small yachts were coming smoothly, behind them. The motor-boats were soon near enough for the crew to see him, and they waved eagerly. Palfrey pointed towards the sinking hull of the launch.

The motor-boats passed him.

One of the yachts drew near, and a man leaned over perilously, and threw a rope. Palfrey gripped it, felt his arm taken in a powerful hold, and was hauled aboard.

He flopped into the bottom of the boat, water streaming from his clothes.

The Chief of Police, immaculate in light grey, stood with his back to a cocktail cabinet in his flat, near the police station, and shook the cocktail shaker vigorously. Off duty, he seemed more blond and vigorous than when on duty; but he was not smiling. Andromovitch sat on a big stool, hugging his knees, and Palfrey in an easy chair.

It was three hours since he had been pulled out of the water. He showed no sign of the ducking, but bleakness, and a cold determination, was in his eyes and the set of his jaw.

'No, we have not found that motor-boat,' said the Chief of Police. It is so difficult. There are hundreds upon hundreds of them in the lakes, it might have come from anywhere. Or again, it might have been stolen—we have inquiries being made about that. If it is possible to find those men, we shall find them.'

Palfrey said: 'I hope so. How's the man in hospital?'

'He will recover, but his face is badly injured.' The Chief of Police stopped shaking, and began to pour out. 'The other—dead.'

'It could, perhaps, have been worse,' said Andromovitch.

The Chief of Police drank, tossing his head back.

'I tell you, Palfrey, it is the worst incident in my career. If they'd killed you . . .'

'Others would have taken over.'

'I cannot understand it,' said the Chief of Police. 'I think that you should leave work of this kind to these others, you should guide and direct . . .'

Palfrey shrugged. 'I wanted to see the Duke. He seems a good chap.'

'He is a great man, the Grand Duke of Nordia. And he will for ever be grateful to you, Palfrey. But that is beside the point. These people have made it clear that they will kill you.'

'It's been tried before.'

'Some might succeed.' The Chief of Police swung round on Andromovitch. 'Is he always like this? A fool of obstinacy?

I want him to have protection while he is in Stockholm, and he refuses. There can be no good reason.'

'Except to see how far they'll go, and find out if we can catch one of them,' Palfrey said. 'You've a nest of them here. Work for you, when I've gone.' He said carefully: 'It's even possible that the woman is somewhere about. How well do you know the islands?'

'As well as most people, but there are so many of them, too many to know them all. I have some men in the lake patrols who have spent their lives in these waters, and there are islands at which they have never touched, islands on which no one has landed, as far as we know. You can be sure, Palfrey, that everything possible will be done to search each one, but—' he shrugged. 'We are trying to find this woman. We do not even know what she looks like—just the sketchy description which Neilssen and the girl Elsa have given us. She is fair-haired, and beautiful—in every town in Sweden, there are a hundred fair and beautiful women!'

'Not all with dark eyes,' said Palfrey. 'Remember Elsa was sure that her eyes were dark. Strange eyes, she said. We want the woman very badly, Kurssen. Desperately.'

'*Everything* shall be done.'

'And you'll let Svenson work with you?'

'Of course.'

'Leave him to report to me, will you?' asked Palfrey.

'Oh, you shall retain your mystery,' said the Chief of Police, with a short laugh. 'But I tell you, I have never been so distressed. If you had been killed in Stockholm——'

'Forget it,' said Palfrey. 'I——'

The telephone bell rang.

The Chief of Police swung round.

'I was not to be disturbed, you understand, unless it was to do with this affair. This could be news!' He snatched up the receiver. 'Yes! Yes, he is here.'

He turned.

'A call for you, Palfrey. Long distance.'

Palfrey took the receiver and stood listening. There were noises on the line, but no voices, no answer when he spoke.

The others sat rigidly watching him.

Then he heard a woman speak in French; a moment later, another woman, in English.

'Hallo, 'Silla!' cried Palfrey.

Two days ago, the Señora Juanita Melano had left Paris. She had made an appointment to see Drusilla, then sent an apology. Drusilla had called at her hotel, to find that she had left hurriedly, two hours earlier; she had gone back to Spain.

'But why on earth,' said Palfrey, 'didn't you tell me before?'

'I did,' said Drusilla. 'I sent word to the airport, you should have had a message when you reached Stockholm. I expected to hear from you, and couldn't wait any longer. There's a story in the evening papers that you were hurt.'

'Wrong man,' said Palfrey. 'I'm fine, darling, are you quite sure about this?'

'Yes, of course—I cabled you care of the airport, and named the time of arrival of the 'plane you were on.'

'Almost inexplicable. But tell me, what are the colour of Juanita's eyes?'

'A strange question! One would have thought you would have remembered.'

'Tell me again, what are they?'

'If it's mere corroboration you want, they are blue-black— very dark. You remarked on them yourself.'

'And her hair?'

'Jet black. Sap, are you all right?'

'No madder than usual, I think. Any news from home?'

'Corny's telephoned each evening—all's well. Are you coming back to Paris, or going straight back to England?'

'London, I think,' said Palfrey. 'I'll fly tonight. Oh, my sweet, I forgot something. When you get to Brett Hall, you'll find another nurse. I mean, governess. Norwegian, speaks excellent English. I don't for one moment think that there's anything wrong with her, and I've——'

'What *are* you talking about?'

'Why, Elsa Olsen! Don't be surprised if you find she turns up, and tell Corny to see that she's made comfortable, will you? But to watch her. I shall stop in London for a day or two, and Elsa should be at the Hall first thing in the morning. Right?'

'I wish I knew what's going on,' said Drusilla.
Palfrey gave a bark of a laugh.
'I wish I did! Goodbye, my sweet.'

Palfrey and Andromovitch slept most of the way to London that night, reached the London airport just after six o'clock, and went straight from there to the house in Brierly Place which was the Palfrey's London home. It was one of a terrace of grey, stately houses in a quiet square, and although many people knew that Palfrey lived there, few knew that it was also the headquarters of Z5.

Some years ago it had been damaged in an attack which had come nearer than anything to extinguishing the brighter lights of Z5; and many of the records had been destroyed. Since then, a Ministry of Works permit had been miraculously obtained, and extensive alterations had been made, especially to the cellar. This cellar extended well into the small garden at the back and beneath the houses on either side, both of which had been taken over by the Department.

There was nothing unusual about the appearance of the house from the outside; the wide, square porch had rounded pillars supporting it, and five steps led to the large front door. Nor was there anything unusual about the spacious entrance hall, the staircase, or the large rooms on the ground floor. But the floors had been reinforced, and the cellar was as nearly bomb and fireproof as anything could be; electrically controlled steel doors could shut it off entirely.

A night and day staff worked there.

Palfrey paid the driver off, and he and Andromovitch went up the steps, letting themselves in with a key. A light was on in a small room on the right, and a man came out—middle-aged, lithe-looking.

'Hallo, Sap!'

'Hallo, Bill,' said Palfrey. 'Still on the watch for bad men?'

'The craziest things can happen.'

'And have they?'

'Not here, but you've been having fun, I'm told.'

'Fun's the word. Food, upstairs?'

'Of course. Good to see you again, Stefan.'

65

'And, always, to see you, my friend.' Andromovitch shook hands.

'Any word from my wife?' asked Palfrey.

'Yes, she reached London late last night and was taken straight out to Brett Hall. She telephoned to say that everything's normal, except that the new governess hadn't turned up.'

'She will,' said Palfrey. He led the way upstairs, walking slowly. It was gloomy in here, even by day. The walls were lined with books, there were a dozen comfortable chairs and, by one of the tall windows, a pedestal desk of the same rich mahogany as the bookcases. This had once been the ballroom, but was now the private office of Z5.

'Nothing changes,' said Andromovitch.

'Only events.'

'Not even those. One challenge to sanity comes, is beaten, and another appears. Sap, you have not been fair to me.'

Palfrey blinked. 'No?'

'You haven't told me everything that's on your mind.' The Russian lowered himself into a huge chair.

'What can I tell you? You can see the possibilities as clearly as I can. The kidnapping of youngsters; drugging them; working on their minds, turning them into—what? Sullen and mature creatures—colloquially speaking, little beasts. When a man like the Grand Duke of Nordia will keep vital facts from the police, he's half-way to playing with the kidnappers. You know all this.'

'It isn't all,' said Andromovitch.

'What else? Juanita? She could just fit in. Madame had been away from Hilsa Island for nearly a week until that day, so she could have been in Paris for the few days before that. Let's say she's a suspect. If we do, we have to answer a pertinent question. Why did she go to those lengths to talk to me?'

'To find out how much you knew,' said Andromovitch, mildly.

'No!' Palfrey was explosive. 'She was telling me to keep a look out for kidnapped children, giving the game away. So it wasn't just curiosity. It could, I suppose, be a ball flung in an opposite direction, keeping Z5 scampering after it while the real villainy is being perpetrated elsewhere.'

'You think so?'

'It's the nearest thing to a reasonable solution that I can make of it,' said Palfrey.

'You have not yet told me what you've done,' said Andromovitch.

'Set the old department working,' said Palfrey. 'I asked Bill Kennedy here to find out all he can about kidnappings, the number of children of between ten and fourteen who've disappeared, in a dozen different countries. The Paris people are working on Dubonnet, we couldn't have done much more in Sweden, you were there when I talked to Rodriquez in Madrid, to check on Juanita and her friends. It'll be a few days before reports come in that will really help us. I've asked . . .' He broke off.

The door opened and a youngish man came in, carrying a tray. Palfrey tapped a corner of the desk, and the man put the tray down, said he was glad to see Andromovitch again, and went out.

The Russian smiled faintly.

'And you are still not being fair,' he said.

Palfrey swung round, strode to the window and looked out into the street. Andromovitch watched him closely, and stood quite still.

'Persistent beggar,' Palfrey mumbled. 'I think you get worse. Merciless, too. Can't I have any thoughts of my own?'

He turned to face the Russian, and Andromovitch was appalled at the pallor which had come to his cheeks and the glitter which had sprung into his eyes; he looked older, and careworn.

'Sap, what is it?'

'My mind,' said Palfrey. 'Going, fast. Stefan, it's eighteen months since a rumour of midget men in midget aeroplanes first started, in the United States. Remember it? Since then, it's cropped up in several places. It nearly outrivalled the flying saucers, at one time. Midget men—midget aeroplanes. Remember?'

'Yes,' said Andromovitch, gently.

'I saw a model that could be of a midget rocket craft, at the Paris garage. A larger one, in the house on Hilsa Island. I've

67

asked the Chief of Police to have it sent over, by air, for examinations. It may be—oh, let us have a race of midgets, from Mars!' Palfrey's voice held a savage note. 'Or Venus, any of the planets. Let's have an inter-global war. Or let's imagine youngsters being trained . . .'

He stopped.

Andromovitch said: ' Why didn't you tell me of this earlier? Then, perhaps, two of us would be crazy. It was never allowed to be reported outside of the Soviet, of course, but there were rumours there. *More* than rumours, Sap. We heard a report on one of these machines, in the Urals—not far from some of the new industrial plants. Spy fever is always running hot with us, and I was sent to investigate. There were the broken parts of a machine, deliberately smashed but not done thoroughly; we could piece it together. It was an aeroplane, a midget jet-propulsion wingless craft, with room for a *very* small man.'

Palfrey said very gently: 'And the man?'

'No trace, except—of footsteps. Footsteps no larger than a child would make.'

10

A Woman of Dazzling Beauty

A WOMAN walked through the gardens of the Louvre, passed
through the archway which led to the Rue de Rivoli, crossed
the road, and entered a car which was drawn up in a nearby
square. The chauffeur drove off immediately, and soon was in
the Place Vendôme, where the cars were parked round the
edges, and the small windows of the jewellers offered fabulous
gems at fabulous prices. She waited, while the chauffeur went
into one of the shops, watched by a commissionaire and two
gendarmes who appeared to have nothing to do, yet who were
interested in the woman.

There was one remarkable thing about her; she was heavily
veiled.

The chauffeur came out, handed her a small packet, then
took the wheel and drove to the Seine crossing at Ile de la
Cité. The powerful limousine passed through the hubbub of
sightseers and sellers of souvenirs, and, on the other side of the
river, stopped in a narrow, sun-baked street.

The woman left the car, and the chauffeur drove off.

The woman was still veiled, but whether the veil hid
imperfections or denied the passer-by the privilege of gazing
on rare beauty, it was impossible to tell.

Reaching a narrow door which opened before she touched
the bell, she stepped inside, nodded to the dwarf who opened
the door, and quickly mounted a flight of stairs. She turned
into a front room and here, for the first time, lifted her veil.

A hunchback stood with his back to the window. He smiled
at her.

69

'Such a day for a veil, Thérèse!'

'It keeps away the dust,' she said carelessly, and smiled back at him. 'How are you, Raoul?'

'I exist when you are not here, and begin to live when you come.' He didn't move, but watched her as she peered into a mirror and tidied her hair. They were the natural things that any woman might be expected to do, but she did them with a grace that even without such remarkable beauty, would have fascinated. When she had finished, she went across to the window and sat down near the hunchback.

But for his back, and his small proportions, he was a handsome man, his dark hair waving from a broad forehead over pleasant grey eyes. He touched her long, slim hand.

'Why do you come to me, Thérèse?'

'I enjoy being here—it is so restful.'

'I am not convinced,' he said. 'What is it you want with me?'

'Serenity and quiet,' she said. 'You are the most serene man I know. Withdrawn from the world, indifferent to its follies, its prides, it humiliations.'

'You make me sound a paragon, or a monstrosity!'

She smiled, and patted his cheek.

'There's no doubt about which it is.'

'You know I love you, Thérèse, and that makes me grotesque.' He touched her hair, then moved away. 'Sometimes I wish you wouldn't come, but if you stayed away, I think I should kill myself.'

'I shall never stay away for long at a time,' said the woman, 'though I shall never be in love with you, or, I think, with anyone.' Her voice was matter of fact, carrying no hurt. 'It is strange that a man of your brilliance should be so indifferent to worldly success.'

The hunchback shrugged.

'Am I so indifferent? I sometimes wonder. I have no passions, Thérèse, except for you, no love of country, no loyalties, little feeling. All were driven out of me when I was a child. There was a time when I hated my fellow men, but . . .' He broke off. 'I am wearying you, you have heard all this before.'

'I like to hear it.'

'To please me.'

70

'No, Raoul.' She shook her head. 'We have agreed that when we talk about each other we shall always tell the simple truth. I like hearing about your past, your struggles. Man is usually a victim of his own emotions, and you are the only one I know who has mastered them.'

'What else was there to do? If I'd tried to go through life among normal people, I should have felt either inferior or superior. I should have cringed and been humiliated, or been bitter and aloof, and in either case been shrugged to one side. So, I schooled myself to indifference; to regard myself as distinct and apart from others, like a creature dropped from another planet.'

She frowned, and moved slightly, then closed her eyes, as if she were content to listen only to the voice, low pitched and of great beauty and repose.

'I've toyed with conceptions which most men laugh at. New worlds, new planets—I've lived my life roaming about them, peopling them with images of myself, and sometimes I almost think that I came from one, instead of from the womb of a woman. I was fortunate, too, there was little my mind would not absorb. When a child, I could startle my teachers with the speed of my grasp of mathematics, my prodigious memory. I could perhaps have become another Dalas, but—.' He shrugged. 'And then by chance, I discovered some simple factors which revolutionised aeronautics, and—I had all the money I should ever need. I could indulge my fancies, play in my dream world.' He laughed softly. 'Then you came into that world, and for the first time in my life I knew what it was to feel emotion. Do you know, there was a time when I hated you for breaking the shell with which I had surrounded myself?'

'So you have told me.'

'It passed,' said Raoul, 'and I discovered that I could have the best of both worlds! I have always appreciated beauty, and always sought perfection in anything I've tried to do, and you are the most perfect thing to look at that I have ever seen.'

'To look at?'

He laughed again.

'Most certainly, my dear Thérèse. Beauty might, possibly does, stop there. What goes on inside your mind—oh, I'm not asking you! I am indifferent, but I know that you can hate.

71

that you are caught up in the vortex of human affairs, lashed by our own violent passions. Those beautiful eyes tell me . . .'
He broke off.
'Yes, Raoul? What do they tell you?'
'Death,' he said, slowly and musingly. 'The light goes out of them. I wonder how that happens? Do you take drugs?'
'Sometimes,' she said lightly. 'I am not, however, an addict.'
'You might become one.'
'I don't think so. What you see is hatred, Raoul—at times I reach a pitch of hatred so great that I have to rest. As now.'
'So you have come because you are troubled again. And I help you. Why should I ask for anything more?'
'The moment you do, you will not be able to help me,' said the woman. 'We have our own separate worlds, mine of hatred, yours of dreams.'
'Dreams sometimes carry the end of reality,' said the hunchback. 'Maybe mine do, and I will be able to conquer space in fact, as well as in fancy. Do you think I am mad, Thérèse?'
'A little mad, perhaps.'
He raised his hand.
'And you, whom do you hate?'
She did not answer.
'You've never told me,' he said.
'I can't tell you. If I were to do so you would associate yourself with my hatreds, and lose that single-mindedness which makes you unique. You've no time to attend to my troubles, to help me—beyond helping me this way. Be satisfied.'
'I'm fully satisfied.'
'You are not.'
He laughed.
'You take me too literally. I am satisfied in this, that we shall be wise to keep our bargain, and satisfied to have you sitting there. After all, one would hardly expect the little pauper hunchback boy to grow up and be so close to the most beautiful woman in the world.'
She laughed, softly. 'You really believe I'm that, don't you?'
'You have a beauty which blinds, fools, dazzles, and deceives men. It is at times unearthly—and you know it as well as I do. You cannot move freely anywhere, unveiled, without causing a sensation.'

'My beauty is the strongest weapon I have,' she said, 'and weapons are best not displayed too often. Raoul, may we have some tea?'

'Of course.'

'And afterwards, will you show me your world?'

'We'll share it,' he said, and rang a bell.

They sat in silence until the door opened and a dwarf, or rather, a midget man, came in. He was perfectly formed, though half the normal size. He wheeled a tea-trolley towards Thérèse, inclined his head, turned and went out.

'In Pierre, you have perhaps the only silent servant in the world,' said the woman.

The hunchback nodded, and Thérèse began to pour out tea.

Raoul led the way out of the room, along a wide passage and then up a flight of narrow stairs. Reaching a landing he pressed a hidden knob, and part of the wall slid away. The opening was narrow, and he went in first.

Thérèse followed him.

They stood on a small platform which jutted out over a huge room, the whole of the top floor of this house and the next. Special steel girders had been fitted to strengthen the roof and walls. It was lighted from below and at the sides, by a form of subdued fluorescent lighting which flooded the fantastic chamber with false daylight.

Above and below, the walls curved, making of the room a gigantic sphere. Small spheres hung within, as if suspended, one of them emitting a fierce red glow.

It was like looking at the universe.

It was a model of the universe.

The world hung in the centre. The woman looked long and earnestly. As she watched, there was a tiny eruption on the surface of the sun.

'I haven't seen that before,' she said.

'It is an improvement—a sun spot breaking out into a hydrogen cloud. There is another improvement—Venus. Do you see?'

She turned towards Venus, and the hunchback watched her intently. She was startled at first, then she smiled and stretched out her hand, touching his.

73

'That is beautiful, Raoul. How did you get the likeness?
From photographs?'

'I need only one picture of you, and I keep it here.' He
touched his forehead, then looked at Venus; the face of
beauty and also the face of the woman Thérèse. She turned
away from it, studying the remainder of the nine planets.

'What other improvements have you made?'

'Several small ones, chiefly in the movement.' Stretching out
his hand, Raoul touched a switch on the wall. The daylight
slowly faded until the only light was the reddish glow from the
sun.

Each of the planets began to move round the sun, at
different speeds.

Thérèse was utterly absorbed. The man did not bring his
hand from the wall but pressed another switch and a tiny
silver dart sped from the earth to Mars, and back again;
moved from there to Venus and so on to all the planets.

'That is how I think inter-planetary communication can be
done,' he said. 'Oh, there are many problems, heat, the density
of the atmosphere, differences of temperature and centres of
gravity, possibly unknown elements. But just as we have
spanned the world, so I believe it will become possible to span
the solar system.'

He led the way to another room on the floor below. Here
there were models of aircraft. The dwarf who had brought in
the tea, was working at some intricate and minute piece of
machinery. Near him was a model of a rocket, about three
feet long.

'And that one *works*,' said the hunchback softly.

'Yes, Raoul, I know.'

He raised his head sharply.

'Thérèse! What do you mean—you *know*?'

'I am quite sure that you would not finish a useless model
with such infinite care,' she said lightly. 'Raoul, who else
comes in here, besides you and Pierre?'

'Just you,' said the hunchback. 'We three, Thérèse, share its
secrets.'

He looked at her, for a long time, and she was the first to
turn away.

11

The Workshops

THE woman of dazzling beauty, whom the hunchback knew as Thérèse Morency, left the house on the north bank of the Seine nearly four hours after she had arrived. Her car was waiting for her. She was veiled as she stepped from the front door, but when she sat back in her car, she lifted the veil and looked up at the window.

Raoul Duval stood there with the shutters open, as he always did when she left. She smiled and sank back in her corner, as if greatly relieved. The car did not return the way it had come, but was driven at great speed to a small town ten miles out of Paris. It was not an attractive town, being dirty and dilapidated. The car turned through the gates of what appeared to be a small factory. It was a sprawling, single storey building, and the sign on the weather-beaten front doors read: *Radio Fabrique—Brun et Fils.* The most noticeable thing about it was the strong wire fence, high enough to daunt the most intrepid climber.

The woman, her veil down again, walked towards a side door, opened it and entered a small office with glass windows, through which the workings of the factory could be seen. A few men were busy, but the time was late, and most of the benches were deserted. A burly man, wiping his forehead as he did so, rose from his chair behind a big, untidy desk.

'You are very welcome, Madame Reine. Good day.'

'Good evening, Philippe.' The woman known here as Madame Reine sat down. 'How is progress?'

'Excellent, Madame!'

75

'There has been no more trouble, I hope.'

'None at all,' said Philippe. 'The other—it was unfortunate but not serious. Even if the police wondered what those strange pieces of metal were, they could not guess. You have been careful, Madame—supremely careful.' His florid face seemed to radiate geniality. 'Think how careful you have been! One hundred and nine parts for these machines, made in one hundred and nine different places. Some by great companies.' He chuckled throatily. 'Some in small garages and factories placed all over France—yes, it is a perfect plan. No one who does not know what the parts are for could guess what is being made of them. You have told me that this is the only place where they are assembled, but I am sure that you would have another, perhaps two or three, assembly plants.'

'Are you?' she asked coolly. 'How many machines are ready?'

'Two more, Madame, and——'

'You promised four.' She did not raise her voice, but it was cold, and there was a deadly look in her eyes; they were cloudy, and strange—a little unnatural.

'Yes, yes.' Philippe rubbed his hands together uneasily. 'There was a slight delay, two of the key men were absent through illness, it was unavoidable. They are working late, you see, by tomorrow they will be ready.'

'Tomorrow is a day late,' she said, 'and I do not like late deliveries.'

'How well I know! But there is nothing I would not do. With my own hands I helped to finish them, to make sure that you would not be disappointed. They are—needed for special work?'

'They are needed,' she said. 'Let me see the two that are ready.'

'At once, Madame!' He sprang to the door and opened it, walking with her to the big factory shop. Electric lamps were burning over the benches where the few men worked, but the rest of the place was gloomy and full of shadows. None of the men glanced up, as they passed, but all turned to look at Madame Reine and Philippe as they went to a door at the end of the factory. This opened to another, larger workship, with

76

a sliding roof, open now to the fading daylight and the first powdering of stars.

'There!' cried Philippe.

He pointed proudly to two machines, larger than the model at Raoul Duval's, but far too small for any known form of aircraft.

The woman went close to one, and opened a small door in the nose of the craft. The interior was the same as that of any normal aeroplane. Every instrument and fitting was in place, the only difference being that all were on a miniature scale.

'Perfection!' fawned Philippe.

'It is what I expect, or I would not employ you,' said Madame Reine crisply. 'And if I did not employ you, you would not have money enough for your little diversions. You know that.'

'I am grateful, Madame.' The man's hands rubbed together obsequiously. 'And I have always served you well, have I not?'

'So I understand. If at any time you fail to do so, then——'
She broke off. 'Philippe, are you sure that when the police searched the garage at the Rue Berthe, they found only the parts?'

'Of course!'

He spoke emphatically, but his eyes shifted uneasily. The woman went to a bench and picked up a small model of the flying machine, identical in size with that which Palfrey had found at the garage.

'How many of these did you make?'

'Only the one, Madame, just the one.'

Her eyes were clouded, as if with doubt. She said abruptly:

'And where is the owner of the garage?'

Philippe shrugged.

'It was not safe to have him loose, Madame, you told me that, and I agreed. He is working here. He lives on the premises with the others, and will stay here until his appearance has been changed and he cannot be traced.' The man chuckled again, deep in his throat. 'You think of everything, Madame!'

'Someone has to,' she said.

'This plastic surgery, it is wonderful. Now, eight men have

come and worked here for a time, and been changed, and—some day it will be my turn. Yes?'

'Philippe, there is one other thing I have to say to you.'

'Madame?'

'Your women.'

'But Madame! I have friends, yes, I do not deny. Madame does not object——'

'I object to anything which may be dangerous, Philippe. You must not see any of them again, until I give you permission.'

Philippe's mouth dropped open, and he backed a pace. She looked at him coldly. His eyes, small and beady, shifted incessantly.

'Do you understand?'

'It—it is most difficult, Madame. Tomorrow——'

'It is because it is difficult, that you must keep away from them,' said Madame. 'I have you watched, Philippe, because I have learned that it is impossible to trust any man. I have discovered that one of these women is taking too much of your time, and you are becoming attached to her. Amusement is one thing, a serious entanglement is another. You will not see her or any of the others again, Philippe.'

'It—it is as Madame says.'

She nodded, and turned away, opening a door on the right of the workshop. Beyond was a small room, with two camp beds, easy chairs, a small stove in one corner; there was a smell of olive oil and garlic. Bending over the stove was a midget man; another, equally small, sat in one of the chairs.

As the woman came in, they sprang round and stood stiffly to attention.

'Are you both ready?'

'At once, Madame!'

'You have your instructions.'

'Of course, Madame.'

'In fifteen minutes you will leave,' she said, and went out.

Fifteen minutes later, to the second, the door opened and the two little creatures came out; now they were dressed in diving-suits, pale grey in colour. They walked briskly, in spite of this cumbrous uniform, going straight to the machines. They did not appear to glance at Madame Reine or Philippe.

Philippe had placed small ladders against the doors, and these they climbed, squeezing into the cockpits. Everything they did was quick and mechanical; they were more like robots than men.

They slid the doors to.

Philippe went to the wall and pressed a button. The pedestal on which the machine was placed moved upwards slowly, until it was just above the opening in the roof.

Both man and woman watched, in growing tension.

Suddenly, the machine was not there.

One moment it had been a glistening spot against the sky, and the next, it was gone, as swift and silent as a lightning flash.

Two minutes later, the other followed.

Philippe pressed the button again, and the pedestals slid back into position, then slowly disappeared, into the floor.

As the couple turned away, there was a sharp sound on the roof; they glanced up. A small boy, dusty hair on end, was gazing down on them.

'Look!' cried Philippe.

'Get him—hold him!' ordered the woman. 'Call the guards!'

The head disappeared.

Three minutes later, the child was caught as he slid down the side of the building, and hurried away.

The woman who was known to Raoul Duval as Thérèse Morency, to Philippe as Madame Reine, left the factory soon after the aircraft had taken off and was driven to a lonely point on the road where another, equally luxurious car was waiting. She changed cars, and was taken back to Paris. When she reached a house near the Quai de Béthune, she was dressed in a different suit, and wore only a filmy veil; it was dark, but under a lamp fastened to one of the walls, she was clearly visible. She did not look the same woman, though no less beautiful.

A woman opened the door of the courtyard for her, and entering, she turned left to a staircase, walked up two flights, and entered her *appartement*. Here she opened a locked door.

79

Sitting on an upright chair, tied with his arms bound to his sides, was Marcel Dubonnet.

The woman said: 'Have you anything more to tell me?'

Wearily, Dubonnet shook his head.

'Why did you go to the garage?'

'I have told you.' The words were little more than a whisper. 'Palfrey told me to look for the taxi, three black wings, one brown. I went to the police, my friend Inspector Blanchard, I found the taxi, I telephoned Palfrey and—was attacked. That is all I know, that is everything.'

The woman went out, without another word.

Downstairs, she said to the woman who had opened the door: 'We do not need Dubonnet further, he has told the truth. Tell them that the body must not be found.'

'Yes, Madame,' said the maid, calmly.

'And tell them to watch Philippe. They know what to do, if he leaves the factory.'

'Yes, Madame,' said the maid.

A crack of thunder deafened Philippe as he stepped outside the factory, later that night. He looked furtively up and down, but if he could scarcely make out more than ten yards ahead, it would be equally impossible for he himself to be seen. The rain lashed down, as he slipped out of the main gates to the garage in which he kept a motor-cycle.

Soon he was driving fast along the pitch-dark roads, chased by the thunder and the lightning. Every now and again, he turned to look behind him, but he did not appear to be followed. Reaching Paris, he left the motor-cycle propped up against the kerb, and walked on briskly. It was still raining, but no so heavily. Lights glowed at a number of windows, but few people were about.

He reached a cul-de-sac, and entered the third house on the right. Once inside, he stood for several minutes, then peered out; no one was approaching. He went slowly up the narrow stone staircase, scanning the dark patches at the landings, but heard no sound. Every now and again he glanced back, but no door opened. At the top landing, he seemed to throw off his nervousness, gave a little throaty chuckle, and let himself in with a key.

'Céleste!' he called 'Céleste, where are you? I am in a hurry, I have something of importance to tell you. Céleste!'

There was no answer.

He took off his coat and stood, smiling happily, for it was not unusual for Céleste to play a game with him. She was a wonderful little woman, Céleste, the most wonderful little woman he had ever met. At forty-five, and so much experienced, he had thought he would never marry, but—he had fallen in love. He, Philippe, was in love.

'Céleste, my little one, I am in a hurry, come out!'

There was no movement.

'Céleste!' His smile faded, not, as yet, anxious, he was a little put out as he stepped through into a tiny kitchen; it was empty, although the light was on. There was one other room, he was a fool not to have gone straight in there; the bedroom. Céleste, of course, was waiting for him.

He swung round, and flung open the door of the bedroom.

Céleste lay on the bed, fully clothed—but with a cord round her neck, biting deeply into the flesh. Her eyes were partly open and her mouth was slack.

'Céleste!' screamed Philippe, and flung himself towards her. 'Céleste!' He reached her and drew her to him, and her head lolled back.

He let her fall.

Her body was warm, but he knew that she was dead.

The vitality seemed to be drained out of his face as he stared at her. Even like that, she had prettiness; her fair hair was freshly done, in the way he liked it, showing her small, pink ears.

'Céleste,' he sobbed.

Then he heard a door open, behind him. A man in the uniform of an *agent de police,* came in.

12

The Silver Flash

PHILIPPE did not move as the agent stepped into the bedroom, looking first at the body of the woman and then at the
man.

Philippe cringed back.

'It was not I, it was not——'

'You are Leon Maillard, sometimes known as Philippe
Panneraude. You strangled a woman in Montmartre on the
night of April 15th, three years ago, another on the night of
August 21st, three years ago, and——'

'No!' gasped Philippe. 'It is a mistake, I am not, I did
not——'

The agent smiled grimly, but his voice changed.

'Will you believe now, Philippe, that there is nothing that
Madame does not know. You have been warned not to come
to Paris, and not to spend time with this woman, who was in
touch with the police, and as a result you have endangered
Madame and all of us. You will come back with me, and in
future——' he drew his forefinger across his throat. 'Only one
thing saves you, Philippe, you are a clever craftsman and
Madame finds you useful. But you lied. Look!'

He pointed with a quivering finger at a shiny, silvery model
of the aircraft, then went across to the bedside table, and
snatched it up.

'Come.'

Philippe did not speak, but gradually lowered his face into
his hands.

The other man stepped forward and slapped him across the
head.

'We are in a hurry. Come!'

Philippe followed slowly, his round, fat face deathly white, and did not look round again at the pitiful thing on the bed.

A woman coming up the stairs saw them and, perhaps because of Philippe's expression, she screamed. Philippe gave a great, bellowing cry, and began to run, while the silver model dropped from his pursuer's hands and rolled down the stairs.

The district was not a dangerous one, but poor and over-crowded. In that little corner, including the cul-de-sac where Céleste lived, there were thirty-odd families. Every one, from the oldest grandmother to the youngest child, was familiar to the gendarme whose duty it was to look after the behaviour of his flock. It was the wife of an ex-pickpocket who indirectly caused the gendarme to visit Céleste's flat, that night.

She sent her oldest child to find him, and twenty minutes after Philippe and the man from Madame had gone, he arrived—short, plump, genial and fatherly, untidy even in his uniform. It was a peculiar little story, of a gendarme who had come out of Céleste's flat with a man who had often visited Céleste. Philippe's cry had terrified the wife of the ex-pickpocket, and after the two men had raced away, she had hurried downstairs. The man drove off on a motor-bicycle, the other in a small car.

The woman had knocked and banged on Céleste's door, and received no answer. She had decided to send for the gendarme whom she knew; the other man had been a complete stranger; what would he be doing in the house?

And so, the body of Céleste was found.

Soon, detectives from the Sûreté were on the scene.

Palfrey sat at the wheel of his Lagonda, and drove towards Brett Hall, Drusilla, his children and—he now knew—Elsa Olsen. In the dashboard pocket of his car was the little model which he had obtained from the garage on the Rue Berthe; and which might or might not prove to be significant. There were moments when he told himself that he was being fanciful; and others, when, remembering Marcel Dubonnet's gasp over the telephone, he convinced himself that it was extremely important.

There had been many reports.

None of those from Stockholm were of much help. Neilssen could tell them no more, no one else appeared to have seen the woman who had owned the house on Hilsa Island—she had, it was said, usually arrived after dark, and what business was it of theirs? A parcel of samples found in the workshop at the house on the island had been sent by air, and Palfrey and the consulting aeronautical engineer of the Department, had spent a long time poring over them; but except that they were parts of a model, larger than that which Palfrey had taken from the garage, but not large enough to be used, it was not of great help.

The aeronautical engineer had been non-committal, and had taken the parts away for further inspection. There was no trace of Dubonnet, in Paris, and the owner of the garage had not been found.

One possibly significant thing was that Señora Juanita Melano had been seen in Madrid on the morning after the disappearance of 'Madame', from Hilsa. The Madrid agent of Z5 reported nothing unusual about her movements, since then. Except for the disappearance of one of her children, she had led an uneventful life since her husband had died three years before. He had been a shrewd and able diplomat; nothing more.

All of these things were in the common way of business. One other was not, and it was constantly on Palfrey's mind, a thing to fear or reject as fantastic, whatever his mood.

From all over Europe, said his agents, there came evidence of the disappearance of an unusual number of children between the ages of ten and fifteen.

It was early evening when Palfrey at last turned between the great wrought iron gates of Brett Hall. As he passed through a belt of beech and oak trees, he could see the house, grey-faced, stately, with its two wings and the centre court, conventionally surrounded by lawns and flowers.

He drove to the centre court, glimpsing Alexander the Second racing round the house in a gale of laughter.

Drusilla appeared, waving happily. Then Palfrey saw her glance up.

84

He followed her glance, and saw a silver flash, remarkable for its brilliance, passing like a comet. As suddenly, it was gone, and he looked away again. Drusilla hurried towards him. 'Sap, it's good to see you.'

'And I pray it always will be,' said Palfrey, kissing her cheek.

She looked with concern at his tired, almost haggard face.

'Candle at both ends,' explained Palfrey lightly. 'Two days down here and I'll be a new man.' He turned with her towards the door. 'How are the children?'

'Excited, because I said you'd be home by bed-time.'

'And Corny?'

'In the study, with Elsa.'

'Which leads,' said Palfrey, 'to Elsa!'

Drusilla was thoughtful.

'She's sweet, but very frightened, Sap. I can't really understand her. She says it's worse now than when you first took her away. She can't forget the other woman, says that it's as if she's watching her all the time. Corny's been a help, and Robina arrived yesterday. They're both trying to cheer her up.'

'Elsa's started to think,' said Palfrey. 'Always a racking experience.'

Drusilla didn't answer, and Palfrey turned to look at the court and the flowers and the beauty of it—and saw another silver flash.

Drusilla started.

'Did you see that, Sap? I've seen it several times, and Corny has, twice. At first I thought I was imagining things—a new kind of flying saucer.'

'Hum,' said Palfrey. 'The old kind's enough to put up with, surely. Hallo, Martin.'

The butler bowed.

'I'm happy to see you here again, sir.'

'Not so happy as I am to be back,' said Palfrey. 'For a golden week-end, Martin, with lashings of food, and I feel I shall want to explore the cellar with you before dinner tonight. Nothing but the best is good enough for a tired man.'

Martin opened the door of the study, which was alongside the great staircase, and the Palfreys went in. Elsa was sitting in a chair by the window when she saw Palfrey, and she

85

rushed towards him, eager, almost beseeching. He took her hands as she searched his face, as if she thought there would be good news there.

'Have you found her?'

'Not yet,' said Palfrey. 'Don't worry, Elsa, you're quite safe here.'

She turned away, the blaze of hope fading from her eyes.

He watched the girl as she stared out of the window; and saw her start. All of them saw the silver speck, which was gone in a flash.

'Again!' cried Elsa. She was trembling.

Drusilla moved forward.

'I'll take her upstairs, Sap.' She put a hand round Elsa's shoulders, and they went out. The door closed, silently.

Cornelius Bruton moved forward from the shadows. The American was smiling faintly, but there was a sombre shadow in his eyes. Palfrey both looked and felt puzzled; he could not understand the way Elsa had behaved, nor Drusilla's start; nor his own sense of dismay. The comparative content he had felt while driving through the park and at seeing Drusilla had gone.

'Well, Corny?' he said.

Cornelius Bruton moved to a chair and dropped into it.

'What's all this, Sap? Bringing the heebie-jeebies with you? I was doing fine until you arrived. Elsa was nearly normal. That's what I guessed, and then——' He broke off.

Palfrey began to play with his hair.

Bruton, married to Drusilla's sister Robina, was, next to Andromovitch, Palfrey's closest friend. Now, his sombre gaze was evidence enough that he, too, was infected by the same disquiet. The worst of the whole thing was the absence of explanation or of reason. Palfrey felt as if he had walked out of the everyday world of certainty and plain, unvarnished facts, into another, darkly perilous. But the sun was shining brightly, and the view from this window could not have been excelled in all England.

Bruton said: 'It's good to see you, anyway.'

Palfrey nodded. The change in his mood had come, he knew, when he had seen Drusilla start as she looked up at the silver streak.

Bruton lit a cigarette. Short, compact and wiry, his thick, iron grey hair had once been almost white, turned from black during one of the affairs of Z5, when he had been held, as hostage to Palfrey; an ordeal from which most men would have died. Something of his strength of body and will showed. Though he had lived in England for many years, he remained as obviously American as Palfrey, just as obviously, remained English.

'How's Stefan?' he asked.

'Eh? Oh—Stefan. Fine. Fine.' Palfrey swung round. 'Sorry, Corny! I don't know what's happened. I've the kind of feeling I used to get when a ten tonner was screeching down from the blue, and I knew I would feel something of the blast, if nothing else. Crazy!'

'Called living on your nerves,' said Bruton. 'But I'm not, and I feel the same way. Sap, when that Norwegian girl reached here, she was just jumpy. She'd been through plenty, and it wasn't surprising. And then she began to get the notion that this woman she talks about was watching her all the time. Could her terror have something to do with the silver streak? She's seen it before, you know.'

Palfrey said slowly: 'Where?'

'At Hilsa Island, I guess. She associates it with the island and the woman. I tried to find out why, but all she would say was that she'd seen it there. Why did you send her here?'

'She's the only person I know who's seen, and could recognise, Madame,' said Palfrey. 'That's why she was to be killed at Hilsa. She's precious.'

'If I were you, I'd get a psychiatrist to have a session or two with her,' said Bruton. 'Sure, I mean it, she's not so good. This last two days she's puzzled me plenty, and I don't think we can deal with her right here.' He forced a laugh. 'Oh, forget it. I want to hear what you've been doing. Everything, and . . .'

Without a moment's warning, a blast struck against the window of the study, with fierce, explosive force. The glass splintered and smashed. Palfrey felt a piece tear into his cheek, dropped to the floor, saw Bruton fling himself forward—and then heard the roar of the explosion. As that faded, there came the thunder of falling masonry.

13

Destruction

PALFREY jumped to his feet and rushed towards the door. He was in the hall before Bruton moved. The rumbling sound continued, and was suddenly broken by a cry; a child's cry, as of fear. It was followed by Drusilla's voice.

'Alex!'

And then there came a scream, as wild as he had heard at Hilsa Island.

Drusilla came tearing down the stairs. The landing windows were smashed, pieces of glass stuck out from the wall opposite, pictures were hanging crookedly, a small bronze statuette lay on its side. Drusilla had fear in her eyes.

'Alex was outside.'

The screaming went on; and the child's crying.

Palfrey turned back into the study, and saw Bruton climbing through the window. He jumped out after the American, and turned to the right. A corner of the house was a mass of rubble, some still tumbling; smoke and dust rose up in a dark cloud, blotting out the sky. Earth and stonework littered the lawns and the flower beds.

'Mummy!' cried the child.

The voice came from the rubble.

Bruton said: 'If he can call out, he's not . . .'

'Marion was there, too,' Drusilla said.

She rushed past Palfrey towards the fallen masonry. The child called out again; but it was the silent child who frightened them; silent and invisible.

'*Mummy!*'

Above the swirling dust rose a small hand. Drusilla stopped and swayed, as if she would fall; for the hand was red with blood. Palfrey pushed past her. With frantic, iron discipline he began to lift the stones away, knowing that one incautious move might bury the child beyond hope or help.

'All right, old chap.' Palfrey's voice was steady. 'We're coming.'

He lifted a heavy stone, and rich dark earth fell from it, showing Alexander the Second buried up to his chest, staring with wild eyes at his father.

'It's all right, we'll soon have you out,' Palfrey said. He managed to lean down, and get his hands beneath the boy's arms. 'Now I'm going to pull; tell me if it hurts.'

He lifted, gently.

'My foot,' whispered the child.

'We'll soon put that right.' Palfrey lifted again, and drew the lad clear.

Drusilla's hands ran lightly, lovingly, over the small body.

Palfrey said steadily: 'Where was Marion, old chap?'

'She—she was with me,' said Alexander. 'We were just coming round to give you a surprise. Daddy, what's happened?'

'I don't know,' said Palfrey.

It was half an hour before they dug Marion out; they found her badly crushed, but breathing.

Drusilla and Robina Bruton were at the hospital; and there had been no report. Elsa was in her room, unconscious from a shot of morphia which Palfrey had given her. A special squad of experts was on the way, to examine the damage and find some indication of the type of explosive which had caused it.

Everyone had been questioned; no one had seen an aeroplane; several had seen the silver flash.

One corner of the house, and half a dozen rooms, were destroyed, but one wing had escaped serious damage. The mass of rubble was being cleared away by the light of car headlamps.

Palfrey and Bruton were in a small room on the other side of the house.

Bruton was walking to and fro. Palfrey sat at a table; he looked—despairing.

Bruton spoke as he walked.

'Listen, Sap, that could have been a time bomb, placed here heaven knows when. You've been shot at before, and this time——'

'All right,' said Palfrey. 'It could have been a time bomb, but I don't think it was. It was an attempt to kill me—or possibly Elsa, because only she can recognise the woman we know as Madame. I should have known that to send Elsa here, was asking for trouble. I have to use my own family as guinea pigs for my own damned experiments. That's what it amounts to.'

Bruton stopped.

'All right,' he said. 'It is your fault. You fixed it. The truth about you is that you ought to take a rest. You've been working at high pressure for far too long, and one of these days you'll go to pieces.'

'It seems, I've already done so,' growled Palfrey.

'Now you're talking nonsense, and you know it. You also know the telephone might ring at any minute, to tell you that Marion's fine.'

Palfrey said sharply: 'Don't be a fool. I've done enough doctoring to know when injuries are serious and when——' He broke off, and jumped up. 'Why the hell doesn't Drusilla call me?'

'She'll call as soon as there's news. Sap, have a Scotch. It'll do you good, and——'

'I prefer to stay sober, and if I start drinking now, I shan't stop,' said Palfrey. He laughed bitterly. 'Oh, you're right enough, I'm suffering from shock—you can even call it hysteria. But there's more to it than that. I'm frightened. I have been for a week or more. The thing you don't understand is always the thing that really gets under your skin.'

The telephone bell rang.

Bruton reached it in three strides and snatched off the receiver.

He waited, looking at Palfrey's glittering eyes.

'Yes,' he said. 'Sure.' He turned away from the mouthpiece, and put the receiver down very carefully.

'Being operated on now. Surgeon non-committal, but there's a good chance.'

'Oh,' said Palfrey.

'Drusilla and Robina are staying at the hospital, overnight. You're not to wait up.'

'Don't be silly,' said Palfrey. 'I'm going to join Drusilla. Of course I'm going to join Drusilla. I was a ruddy fool to let her go alone.'

'She wasn't alone, Robina was with her. Sap, you won't be one blessed bit of good to her if you don't get some rest. You haven't slept for two or three days, have you?'

'I've slept.'

'Not enough.'

Palfrey said thinly: 'I'm going. Care to come?' He turned towards the door, and as he reached it, the telephone bell rang again. Palfrey pressed a hand against his forehead, and spoke in a more natural voice. 'Sorry, Corny. I can't get the disappearing children out of my mind. They haunt me. I had to wait to see if we could get some lead from the mess, but there's nothing. You stay. If anything crops up, you can call me at the hospital and I can be back in less than an hour.'

'Sure,' said Bruton, and lifted the receiver. Yes?'

Palfrey went into the passage beyond.

'Hold on!' cried Bruton, and then shouted: 'Sap, come back. Hurry!' He spoke into the mouthpiece again, and when Palfrey reached the door, there was a glint in Bruton's eyes. 'Sure,' he said. 'Okay, I've got it. Okay, Stefan, I'll tell him right now.'

He banged down the receiver.

'Stefan?' Palfrey said abruptly.

'That's right. From Paris. They found a murdered woman last night, and also found a model of the midget machine that's on your mind. A child found it at the foot of the stairs, and thought it was a toy. A policeman was curious, I guess, and it turned out a man who ran away from the flat dropped it. The police think they can find out where it was made.'

'Well, well,' said Palfrey.

'You stick around,' said Bruton. 'I'll hop over to Paris.'

Palfrey said: 'Wait a bit, Corny.'

91

It was touch and go with his daughter, and there was no way of telling whether she would pull through. Drusilla was with her, and not alone; yet she would feel solitary and lost without him. He had to measure the discovery in Paris against this; and add his compelling conviction that he was on the fringe of some great horror. He was not just a man with a man's full rights; he had surrendered those to Z5. But there were moments when the surrender brought him close to revolt. Was there anything he could do in Paris which was beyond the scope of Bruton and Andromovitch?

He stood quite still, with his fingers on the door.

He remembered that silver streak and everything that had gone before; the sleeping children and the story of the illness they had suffered, and how they had changed. Elsa's screaming was in his ears, vying with Drusilla's desperate cry after the explosion and her look when she had known for certain that Marion was beneath the rubble.

He could help Drusilla by being with her; but he could not help Marion.

Was he needed in Paris?

Palfrey walked agitatedly across the room.

'We'll both go,' he said, in a different voice. 'Will you fix the aeroplane? I'll arrange to have Elsa taken away from here, and looked after somewhere else. She'll have to be taken out carefully. I——'

He broke off abruptly.

'Puzzle,' he said. Something isn't working in the brain-box. If that was an attack on Elsa, then they know that she was brought away. Can they know? Or was it another crack at me?' He didn't frown, and strangely, he looked less haggard. 'We'll find out.'

Twenty minutes later, they were on the way to London Airport.

Stefan Andromovitch stood in the room where the dead woman had been found. On the bedside table was a little ebony mount, and it was obviously the thing on which the model of the machine had been mounted; the machine, which had retractable wheels, fitted perfectly on to it.

'There can be little doubt about this, Sap,' Andromovitch said. The police have told me that the man who came to see Céleste is wanted for murder, and disappeared some time ago. He once lived in Montmartre. One of the police thought he recognised the man, who was on a motor-cycle, near this street.

'And there is this. A neighbour saw it some time ago and greatly admired it—is it not beautiful?' He held up the tiny model, and looked at it thoughtfully. 'Céleste told her that this man had made it for her, he is an engineer; a very clever precision engineer, who was mixed up with a bad set—that is right?—and after a quarrel, killed the woman for whose murder he was wanted. He is suspected of other crimes, too.

'He is being sought, and there is a chance that he will soon be found, because the police have traced that motor-cycle to a small town, ten miles out of Paris. There is, of course, nothing in this room that will help.'

Palfrey said: 'No. It's a pretty thin line.'

'Thin? We are looking for a brilliant engineer, Sap. I have told the police of this small town to expect us, and Corny is already on the way,' said Stefan. 'Shall we go, my friend?'

They went downstairs. Three cars were parked in the cul-de-sac, and half-a-dozen gendarmes were on guard. Further away, Jules Santot was talking and gesticulating to another man. Santot's tie was loose, his collar undone at the neck, he looked as if he were playing a Bohemian in a film. Palfrey smiled faintly as he stepped towards the car. Doing so, he saw, more fully, Santot's companion. He stopped so suddenly that Andromovitch bumped into him.

'See that chap talking to Jules?'

Andromovitch glanced up, piercingly.

'I have seen him, yes, but I do not recall where.'

'I pointed him out to you, in Stockholm,' Palfrey murmured.

'But yes, of course, I recall him now. Gustav, son of the Grand Duke of Nordia.'

'That's right.' Palfrey turned away from the car as Gustav of Nordia rushed forward.

'Palfrey, I've got to see you!'

'Well, here I am. How did you know I was here?'

'I telephoned your home. I was told that you had left for

Paris, and I was walking along the Boulevard de la Madeleine when I recognised you. I knew it was you, but this imbecile tried . . .'

'Just a minute,' Palfrey said. He was aware of the gaze of the little crowd within earshot. He did not look round, but found himself wondering whether anyone in it was more than a spectator; whether any had followed him. He could not forget the possibility that someone knew that Elsa Olsen was at Brett Hall; that was the only reasonable explanation of the attack on the house. 'Why did you come to Paris, Gustav?'

'To see you. You came from here, you told my father that, I thought perhaps you'd come back.'

'Shrewd thinking. Why so anxious?'

'You promised you'd consider letting me help.'

'Well, Paris offers plenty to do,' said Palfrey, temporising.

'But I want to help find that damned woman who kidnapped my sister!'

'A worthy objective,' said Palfrey. 'Gustav, I can't wait now. I don't know how long I'll be tonight, and may not be free until the morning. Where are you staying?'

'I arrived in Paris only this evening, I have not yet arranged an hotel.'

'I see. Then go to the Hotel Nicolas, Rue St. Germain—tell them that M. Santot asked them to find you a room, and wait there until you hear from me.'

The Swede's eyes glowed. 'You'll let me help?'

'Probably.' Palfrey turned on his heel, and went back to the car, but he spared time for a glance at Santot. The glance conveyed the message that Santot expected, but did not greatly relish; he was to follow the young Swede.

'At this rate,' said Palfrey, 'we'll never get out to the garage.' He sounded almost peevish as he climbed into the car. 'Curious, Stefan. I wonder if——'

'There is time for wondering later on,' said the Russian.

Palfrey smiled. 'And yet, you know, I'm glad he turned up. It's something else to think about. Just for safety, I told Kennedy at Brierly Place to get all the information he could about the Nordias and the parents and relatives of the four kidnapped children. Just one of many jobs that seem a waste of time, but might prove useful.' He sounded almost content.

Their police chauffeur drove at speed along the wide, straight road towards the town where Philippe was believed to have kept his motor-cycle. As they neared the town, they saw a red glow in the sky, but before they commented on it, Palfrey saw something else; a silver streak, like a star, which appeared and was gone in the same flash. He grabbed Andromovitch's arm.

'See that?'

'The streak, yes.'

'It was the same streak that we saw at Brett Hall,' Palfrey said abruptly. 'Brighter, in a way, and yet——'

A sheet of flame split the sky and the earth some distance ahead of them, and fast upon it came the roar of an explosion.

14

The Children

FLAMES shot up from a building which they could not see, and the sky was filled with a lurid glow. Palfrey leaned forward and hissed into the driver's ear:

'Faster—faster!'

The man trod on the accelerator, and the car shot forward. As they neared the town, they could see the gaunt outline of the steel girders of factory buildings, clear against the flames. People were standing at their doors, astonished, incredulous, coloured vividly by the glare.

A car lay, upturned across the road, blown there by the explosion. Now they could see the flames and hear their roar; and see a dozen or so people near the factory, their hands shielding their eyes. It was a fierce heat, and there seemed to be a core of white in the ball of red fire.

Palfrey leaned forward again, but he did not need to tell his driver to stop.

As Palfrey and Andromovitch climbed out, heat seemed to strike at them. Opposite the blazing factory was a garage; or what was left of a garage, and Palfrey had no doubt that it was where Philippe had left his motor-cycle.

A man came out of the crowd of surging rescuers. It was Garon, the agent with whom Palfrey had worked in the Rue Berthe.

'Anything?' asked Palfrey abruptly.

'Two explosions,' said Garon abruptly. 'The first started the fire, the second added to it. It is not likely that anything will be salvaged.'

A gust of wind blew the flames towards them. Two gendarmes moved across, recognised Garon, saluted and moved on. Few people were near, except the officials; the fire and the explosion had frightened them too much for casual gaping.

'Can we get hold of some people who worked at the place? Or who knew it well?' asked Palfrey urgently. 'And after that we must track the owners.'

They found eleven men, that night, who worked at the factory which, under the name of *Radio Fabrique—Brun et Fils*, had flourished. None of them knew anything about the owners of the factory. Most had seen only a heavily veiled woman in conference with Philippe, the works manager. Skilled engineers, they were engaged in making special parts believed to be for a mysterious form of radio; it was, they said, very secret; Philippe allowed one group of men to make one section, second and third groups to make others. They knew that the radio was assembled in another workshop of the same factory, and one of them knew that component parts for this mysterious set were delivered from all over France, and some, in fact, from outside the country. Although everything was so secret, there was a general conviction among the men that the finished object was a new and revolutionary form of television set.

No one hinted at an aircraft or other machine.

The assembly men lived in a house owned by the company, working together, and in no way mixing with the other workmen. The security precautions had been as great as any used by the occupying power during the war.

It was taken as a matter of course, in the town; everyone knew about it, and the television invention was an 'open' secret. The local police were well aware of it; they had no reason to be suspicious. Let the fools think it *was* a secret! For instance, the works manager was never seen in the little town, he always arrived in a closed car or after dark. It was known that he had a mistress, that sometimes he went off at night on a motor-cycle; but they did not know that he had been wanted for murder.

The house in the factory grounds, in which the assembly men had lived, had been the first to be gutted. Here, also, the highly skilled technical staff had lodged.

It was a great tragedy; a terrible tragedy. No one knew how many people had perished. No one knew, either, how the holocaust had started.

The fire was burning low, and the first light of dawn was spreading across the sky, before Palfrey had finished interrogating the men. He did not feel tired, but was glad of the fresh air and of the coffee which a hospitable Captain of the Police obtained for him.

Fire brigades from Paris and neighbouring districts had been at work for several hours, and the seriously injured had long since been taken into hospital. Some of the rubble in the badly damaged streets was already being cleared up. There was, as yet, no estimate of the number of casualties. Palfrey asked himself why he did not feel tired; why he was filled with a curious inward excitement. This, the latest move in the affair, could hardly be called a success.

Yet it was a success; no one else would argue that the explosion at Brett Hall had been a coincidence; no one would seriously argue with him, now, that there was no association between the explosion and the streak in the sky; no one, that was, with whom he had discussed it.

For the streak in the sky was a phenomenon which had often been seen in this town. No one had paid it much attention; it was natural that when a highly-powered receiving set was being made, as at the factory, there would have to be powerful generators and dynamos; what was surprising in a few flashes?

There was one question he had not yet asked; whether anyone had noticed unusually small men in the factory, or approaching or coming away from the hostel. Deliberately he kept that question back, waiting for someone to volunteer the information.

A car stopped outside the police station, and Palfrey saw Andromovitch stepping out of it. Seeing Palfrey, he turned and hurried towards him.

'Sap, come quickly.'

Palfrey was alerted in a flash.

They hurried back to the car, and leapt into it. Without a

98

word, the police driver restarted the engine. They passed the factory, and the crowds now gathered round the fire engines, past the powerful jets of water which were being poured on to the still smouldering wreckage, and then turned between the gates of a house hidden from the road by a high wall.

The building was tall, and dilapidated.

Andromovitch led the way into it without a word, Palfrey following. Garon was there, he saw, with several gendarmes and plainclothes men; and on all their faces was a strained look which almost matched Stefan's.

'Upstairs,' Andromovitch said.

The stairs were old, and creaked at every step. At the top, Andromovitch turned abruptly, and touched a door.

'In here,' he said. 'Be prepared, Sap, you won't like it.'

Palfrey stepped inside.

It was a long, high room, wide enough for beds to be placed opposite each other against the walls. On each, lay a child; quite still. But they were not sleeping, they were staring towards the ceiling, unaware, unnoticing.

Andromovitch said: 'And now, follow me again.'

Palfrey felt a sickening sense of nausea, because of the expressions on the children's faces; their set stare, their pallor, and their silence.

Andromovitch opened another door, and Palfrey stepped through, prepared to find worse; and instead, he found something much better. This was a smaller room, and here were only a dozen beds. Clustered togther were nine or ten excited children of both sexes, whispering among themselves. As Palfrey appeared, they fell silent; but this was the silence of normal children. Near them was an elderly man, sitting on one of the beds.

'That is a doctor from the town,' said Andromovitch. 'He has examined those in the first room, and can make nothing of them. These, he says, are quite well and happy. But there is one room where it is much worse.'

Palfrey was about to say: 'In what way?' but realised he would know soon enough, perhaps too soon.

Andromovitch led the way to a narrow passage, off which opened three more doors. Two gendarmes stood outside one of them. They looked almost as pale as the motionless children in the big room.

The quiet was broken by a piercing scream, which was cut short; but it came again. The gendarmes flinched. Palfrey moved towards the door, and opened it. As he stepped into a small room, the scream came again. He stood with a hand on the door, and his heart seemed to stop. There were seven or eight beds, and on all but one a child lay tossing and turning restlessly; on the last, a boy was standing up, stretching his arms towards the ceiling. His eyes were blazing, his face was the face of a maniac. He screamed suddenly, and leapt convulsively up and down, up and down.

As Palfrey walked forward the boy sprang off the bed and rushed at him. Andromovitch tried to intercept the child, but the boy eluded him, and leapt at Palfrey. Palfrey thrust out his arms, but the force of the rush was too great, he felt the small hands claw at his face, then fingers clutched at his neck, tightening, choking the life out of him.

Andromovitch seized the boy's arms, but with a superhuman wriggle the boy twisted free and sprang at the Russian. He succeeded in forcing Andromovitch back a few paces, before he was caught and held fast in those great hands.

Palfrey fingered his own throat, gingerly.

The boy opened his mouth wide, his face distorted, gave one piercing scream, then became limp. Andromovitch lowered him gently to the floor, and looked down at the pale face and the lids which had closed mercifully over the blazing eyes.

The boy was dead.

It was believed that the house was an asylum for mentally sick children. It had been in use for a little over six months. It was known that at least seven children had died there, but most, it was understood, had been discharged as cured. The staff came from some other district, but all had gone when the police arrived.

Downstairs, in a pleasant room with the windows open to admit the morning sun, Palfrey sat with Andromovitch, watching the bees flying about in the garden, the stirring of the flowers, the brightness of the grass. They had been told

100

by one of the cleaning women that this room had been used by the resident doctor and matron, whose descriptions had already been sent to Paris for general circulation throughout France; and to London.

'What made you come here?' Palfrey asked.

'The quest for small people,' said Andromovitch. 'It was a mistake, Sap—my French is not good. I looked for small men and was told I would find them here—and this is what I found.'

'The doctor and the resident staff had gone then?'

'It is said that they disappeared, early this evening; there was a great to-do, and many papers were burnt, and then three cars arrived and took them away. I——'

He broke off as a little group turned into the drive from the road. An oddly assorted group; two gendarmes, a man and a woman, a small child in her arms and another, holding on to her hand. The group walked vigorously towards the house, and Palfrey went into the hall, to greet them.

They were not interested in Palfrey, but he understood what they wanted. The man and woman had lost their elder boy, a few days before. It had been rumoured that children had been found here who were *not* sick, they wished to see the children, in the hope that they could identify their son.

The gendarmes on guard turned to him.

'Yes, of course,' said Palfrey. 'Let her see them.'

There was no need to take her through the room of silent children, and he led her to the second room, where he had seen the happy, normal group. As he watched the woman, he saw her coarse face suddenly brighten with joy. She released the toddler and, hugging the babe to a vast bosom, rushed forward with her free hand outstretched. One of the boys in the little group gave a shout of delight, and ran towards her. Mother, babe and twelve year old seemed to disappear in a billowing mass of clothes.

Ah! but Pierre was a wicked son, to desert his mother and father, he did not deserve such good parents. It was wrong, it was wicked, to be so venturesome. One day he would not be so lucky—look where his pranks had led him. To a home for imbeciles!

The child protested: 'But they would not let me come back! They tried to kill me, but I hid.'

'Lies you tell me! Oh that your good father and I should be cursed with such a fool of a child! Never again will I——'

'Madame,' said Palfrey, and his gentle voice stemmed the flood of words. 'May I talk to Pierre?'

'But yes, perhaps he will heed your scolding more than mine.'

Palfrey smiled, and led the child aside.

Pierre, a little scared, walked meekly with Palfrey to the front room.

'Don't be frightened, Pierre. Sit down.' Palfrey waved towards a chair. 'Your mother is very worried, you understand, and she does not mean all that she says. Now, you can perhaps help me. I am a policeman.'

'So!' The boy's eyes rounded.

'Yes, and you may be able to help the police. Just tell me what happened.'

The boy said excitedly: 'I climbed over the wire fence of the factory. It is the highest fence for many miles. It was to see the wonderful television. I said I would get into the grounds, but the other boys laughed at me and said it was impossible——'

He broke off.

Palfrey said gently: 'Did you see the television, Pierre?'

'No—no, sir.' Pierre looked down at his feet, and his hands were moving, twisting and twining.

'What did you see?'

'It—it was nothing, sir.'

'Pierre, you promised to tell the truth.'

The boy hesitated, not sure whether he would be believed, not even sure whether he wanted to be believed, then spoke in a nervous rush.

'Well—I climbed on to the roof. It was nearly dark, sir. I climbed on to the roof, and——'

He broke off.

'Go on,' said Palfrey. 'It might be very important.'

Andromovitch was leaning back in his chair, watching the lad intently.

'I saw two strange machines,' said Pierre nervously. 'They

102

were very bright. And there was a man and a woman—a beautiful woman—and two creatures who climbed *into* the machines.' He paused, but it was with the excitement he was recalling; and Palfrey waited until he went on, unprompted.

'They were there below me, sir, like shining silver, and—one came up as high as the roof, and stayed there for a moment, so bright that it almost blinded me; and then—it was gone. *Gone*,' he repeated hoarsely, and then jumped up and cried: 'It is true, what I tell you, it is true!'

15

How Many

AT THE house in Brierly Place, on the following afternoon, there was more excitement than usual. Kennedy, the man in charge of the headquarters of Z5, and his staff, called it another 'invasion of V.I.P.s'. In all, about twenty men arrived.

They gathered in the big library on the first floor, sitting round a table like directors at a board meeting. There were representatives from France, the United States, Russia, Great Britain, and from groups of other countries. At the head of the table sat Palfrey, and near him Andromovitch.

Palfrey smiled round at the high personages about him.

'Very good of you all to come, gentlemen. I propose to lose no time in getting down to facts. There are a lot of them to report.' He paused a minute, then raised his head, and raked everyone present with a searching gaze. 'It is a long story, and I think you should know everything that led up to it.'

Speaking quietly and deliberately, he told them what had happened; how it had begun, how it had developed. He told them of the disappearance of the children, of the model, the silver streaks, the explosion, and the fires. He did not once raise his voice, or lose his grip on the audience.

After a while, he reached the affair near Paris, and the child who had died; and Pierre, who had been so daring and had seen so much.

He stopped.

There was not a sound in the room. All faces were pale and harassed, the reflected horror of those who had listened to a tale of almost unbelievable corruption and depravity.

An American said: 'Have you added all this up, Palfrey?'

Palfrey's hand strayed to his hair.

'We can reach a provisional total of results and we can ask pertinent questions,' He paused. 'First, that there is this aircraft, much smaller than any known, rocket-like in construction and undoubtedly rocket propelled, although much more controllable than any known rocket today. Undoubtedly it travels at supersonic speed, and there is little doubt that it is capable of piercing the stratosphere—I have received the most detailed reports from aeronautical experts, and they all agree that the speed is supersonic and the machine capable of flying through the stratosphere. What we don't know is—how many are in existence, and who is behind the project.'

A Frenchman said heavily: 'How many machines were there?'

'The final reports from the search of the wreckage came in yesterday, and as far as it's possible to tell, there were two machines. Among the wreckage was molten metal of a kind not widely known—in fact, an alloy, extremely strong and very light. Examination showed that two heaps of this molten metal were large, suggesting that it came from a finished or a nearly complete machine. Other heaps were much smaller, suggesting parts in preparation. We have found no trace of anyone who can tell us anything about the number being assembled at the plant, but the evidence of the boy Pierre suggests that two had been finished and left the factory a few days before the fire; which means that four had been assembled about the same time. We have no idea whether forty or four hundred are in existence.'

'Four hundred!' exploded the representative from the Foreign Office. 'Do you seriously suggest——'

'The factory has been making these supposed television sets for over a year,' said Palfrey. 'There is no reason to believe that there was only the one factory; I think we shall find that this was one of several. The wisest thing is to assume that several hundred of the machines are in existence.

'There's another thing.

'The first report of a midget aeroplane and a midget pilot is now nearly three years old. Reports have come from all over the world, including the Soviet Union. The entire number

105

of reports received to date is one hundred and seven.'

When he stopped, there was a hush in the room. Every eye was turned towards him, and no one moved.

'We then have to look at the second factor,' Palfrey said flatly. 'That is, the explosive used. It is an extremely powerful one—*not* atomic, gentlemen, we have that to be thankful for! —and a small quantity can be extremely destructive. The weight of the bombs dropped at Brett Hall and in Paris have been estimated at one hundred pounds; the effect is as great as that of a ten-ton bomb made of ordinary high explosive. We have no idea how many of these bombs are available, but the wise thing is to assume that there is an unlimited quantity and that they can be used aggressively at any time, and in a way against which there is no known defence.'

He uttered the last words very softly, to an audience, by now, incapable of showing any emotion other than stunned acceptance.

'This is a completely new situation,' Palfrey went on. 'I have received information from all the experimental aeronautical stations throughout the world. There is no indication of any kind that any machine now under construction has the manipulative dexterity, range, or speed of these little things; which means that we've no defence against them yet. It is a fact which I think we have to accept, that they exist in sufficient quantities to be extremely dangerous—and there is no way of telling where an attack might fall. Also, there's no indication that attacks are intended, except as defensive measures. Both of those we've known about have been defensive—to prevent us from talking to the Norwegian girl, and to prevent us from finding the factory undamaged.'

'Have you any idea who is behind it, Palfrey?' the American asked.

'No. There are the reports of this woman of unusual beauty. She was undoubtedly on Hilsa Island. The boy, Pierre, has described her, and his description tallies with that given by Elsa Olsen. We've nothing else to go on. It is possible but unlikely that Juanita Melano is associated with her. At one time I thought it possible that they were one and the same, but the Señora was undoubtedly in Madrid when the woman was seen by Pierre—and even at supersonic speeds, you

106

can't be in two places at the same time.' Palfrey smiled faintly. 'That's probably the worst angle, from the military point of view. The other—' he shrugged. 'I think I like it even less.' 'Yes, the children,' said the Belgian representative, very gently. 'What can you tell us about them?' 'A little. As far as we can judge, the children are subjected to a treatment which first demands considerable sleep and then the injection of a drug which makes them ill. They run high temperatures, and the symptoms are all those of cerebral meningitis, with a few variations. Undoubtedly the drug has an effect on the mind. Some subjects are unable to stand the treatment, and go mad. There is little doubt that these die. As far as I can tell, those who come through are completely changed. We have the evidence of Elsa Olsen on the one hand, and the evidence, partly circumstantial, of those at the nursing home near Paris. Those children who were ill when I saw them three days ago, have passed through the crisis now. I have been talking to the medical expert who went there at my request. He says that the children show signs of sullenness, hostility and maturity; they appear to have the minds of grown men. The recovery appears to be extremely fast. Physically, they are weak but showed signs of developing considerable mental strength. The indications as I see them are that these children become adults, to all intents and purposes, and also of a temperament which makes them malleable in the hands of their masters. I should say that the machines are piloted by them, after they have been through a toughening process and a training which makes them physically able to cope. I should say, also, that one of the effects is to make them indifferent to ordinary fear—I say indifferent deliberately, because that means they are likely to take risks without thinking, and to be unimpressed by physical danger.

'We come, gentlemen, to the inevitable question; how many of these adult children are there?

'We have little indication, but we know that several hundred have been treated at the nursing home we discovered; a dozen in all, at Hilsa Island. Again, we have to assume that there are many other centres of treatment. I have collated figures from all over the world, showing the number of children between the ages of ten and fifteen who have disappeared in

107

the past twelve months. The total as far as I can judge, is a little over eleven thousand.'

He stopped again. The American stood up abruptly, and his chair crashed back to the floor. The thud was loud, several of the others started violently. The American, tall and angular, moved round the room to the window, and stood looking out.

'Eleven thousand,' Palfrey repeated. 'It's an axiom that if you can take control of the children, you control the future of the nation. It's been applied in different ways a hundred times. We've known of children taken over by the state authorities and, over years, turned into fighting machines without heart, conscience or human feeling as we understand it. In the past, it has taken years, and now a way has been found to shorten the period—probably to a few months.

'Well, gentlemen, that is the situation. My agents are working all out to find other centres, and we have the co-operation of most governments. After today, I'm sure that everyone will give us all the help they can. That is why this meeting was necessary. Er—there is one more thing.'

'Yes?' That was the Dutchman.

'I talked about there being no defence. There's one, of course—our old friend, attack. If we can find these centres and the people concerned, we shan't have trouble. In fact, we'll have made a lot of progress in aeronautics, and could turn that to our advantage. The danger is that now the counter attack has developed and the people concerned find themselves in danger, they might decide to attack themselves, and we have to be prepared for that. But however many machines are available, I think we can be sure that any attack would be on a limited scale. It might be heralded by some kind of ultimatum. We have no idea what is intended, of course. Almost the only thing we know for certain is that no *nation* is involved. One good thing, we can pull together on it.'

He looked at the representative from the Kremlin; and the man nodded, heavily.

'And what do you want of us?' asked the American.

Palfrey shrugged. 'Prompt co-operation everywhere and, I'm afraid, more money. Probably a great deal of money. We shall need to use the intelligence services of the world, and there must be no delay.'

108

After a pause, the American said: 'There'll be no delay. Anything else?'

'Nothing,' said Palfrey gently, 'except to thank you gentlemen for your united support.'

After seeing the last of his guests off the premises, Palfrey returned to the big room, where Andromovitch sat with a set of cards laid out in front of him.

'Satisfied, my friend?'

Palfrey moved restlessly.

'How I hate waiting, inactivity! We're bound to get some reports in soon. Did I tell you I had Gustav of Nordia brought over to London?'

'A most persistent young man.'

Palfrey shrugged. 'Strange that he should have found me so quickly. I supose he could have seen me in the car, by chance. On the other hand——'

'His own sister was involved,' said Andromovitch.

'Yes,' said Palfrey. 'But there is one unpleasant feature I didn't stress at the meeting. It is this: We have no idea how long this business has been going on. It could have started years ago, and it could well be that there are a large number of young people, in influential families, who've already been treated and have been trained to show all the normal reactions. Gustav is twenty-three; Elsa, she says, twenty-one. When we're dealing with the young, we don't know whom we can trust, do we?'

Andromovitch said slowly: 'You have a devilish mind, Sap.'

'To catch a devil one must first understand how a devil thinks,' said Palfrey gravely.

The woman of great beauty sat at a hotel window, overlooking the lake at Lucerne. Now and again she smiled, as if at some secret joke.

It was early afternoon, on the day following Palfrey's session with the people of importance.

The room was large and beautifully decorated; one of a suite of three.

She had been sitting there for half an hour when a door

opened and a man came in. He was quite young—twenty-two or three, perhaps, and of normal size, yet there was something about him which suggested abnormality.

'I have the reports, Signora Bianchi.'

'Tell me,' she said.

'At once, Signora. There was complete destruction at the factory. The authorities have, of course, been investigating closely, and it is probable that they have traced the alloy, and have some idea of how many machines were being assembled. It is known that no plans or details were discovered, and they have not captured any of the assembly plant workers, most of whom were killed in the explosions and the fire which followed. It is established that Palfrey obtained two models of the machine. Each was made by the man, Philippe, one presented to his mistress and one to the owner of the garage on the Rue Berthe, who was making certain parts of the machine. The owner of the garage was one of those who died.'

The woman nodded, but did not speak.

The young man continued in the same smooth voice:

'The girl, Elsa Olsen, has been removed from Palfrey's home in Buckinghamshire, and has not been traced.'

'Not?' the woman's voice was sharp.

'I regret to say so, Signora.'

'Go on.'

'In Paris, Gustav, son of the Grand Duke of Nordia, was seen with Palfrey, and afterwards watched by one of Palfrey's men. This man took him to a hotel where, it is believed, Palfrey and some of his men meet when they are in Paris. He was afterwards sent to London, where he is staying at a small hotel in Kensington. It will be recalled,' added the youth softly, 'that Gustav of Nordia was a patient of yours, Signora.'

'I do not forget.'

'I beg your pardon. As he has not been used, it occurred to me that you may have decided that it was not successful, since he was subjected to the treatment in the early stages. I was with him myself.'

'I am asking for your report, not your recollections.'

'Yes, Signora. Palfrey and the Russian, Andromovitch, have been in London—but Andromovitch left last night, by air, for an unknown destination. It is believed, but not known for certain, that he has been discussing the situation with aeronautical experts, including those who are experimenting with stratopheric aircraft. Bruton, the American, is still in Paris.'

'Doing what?'

'Making visits to many garages and small factories, but as yet there is no report of a visit to one of ours. The danger now, Signora, is that when he finds a factory which has been supplying *Brun et Fils,* he will make some limited discoveries.'

'It is obvious that in time they will discover all the parts which go to make the machine, and as they are not fools, eventually assemble one.'

'The manufacturers could be—destroyed, Signora.'

'That will not be necessary. Those factories making integral parts will be destroyed, the others will remain. What else?'

'Yesterday, there was a meeting at Palfrey's London headquarters, when many representatives of various nations attended, and it is certain that he made a full report. It is equally certain that, since he came upon the nursing home with the children, he made good use of his discoveries there.'

He stopped. For the first time, the woman turned to look at him. Her face was quite expressionless.

'This Palfrey must go.'

'Yes, Signora, but very humbly may I suggest that even if the one man were to be killed, there are others. It is not an individual we need fear——'

'*Fear!*' She spat the word at him. '*Fear*? How dare you use the word to me. Are you telling me that you are *frightened?*' She struck at him. He stood stiffly to attention, looking at her but showing no resentment. She struck at him again and again, but tired at last of his impassivity. Red weals showed livid on his white face. She said coldly: 'If you repeat that mistake, I shall know what to do. Go.'

He bowed stiffly, turned, and went out of the room. As he disappeared, the woman glared towards the door, her beauty entirely destroyed by the insensate fury which took possession of her. She did not move for what seemed a long time; but gradually her expression changed.

Another door opened and Raoul Duval, the hunchback, stepped into the room.

16

The Gentle Hunchback

AT SIGHT of him the woman started, her hands raised
to her breast, staring as if she could not believe her eyes. The
hunchback stepped towards her, making hardly a sound. He
stood two yards away, looking into her face, and it was
impossible to read his expression.

'Raoul! This is delightful.'

'And so, my dear Thérèse,' said Duval gently, 'you begin to
lie to me, although we had agreed that there should be no lies
between us. You are appalled to see me.'

'Surprised, Raoul, certainly.'

'Appalled,' he repeated. 'And why not, Thérèse? You did
not know that I knew you as the Signora Bianchi. You did
not think I should ever find you here, or anywhere but at my
house.'

She stretched out a hand.

'Now that you are here, come and sit with me, Raoul.
Already I feel better for seeing you.'

'Tell me, how often do you lose your self-control like that,
Thérèse?'

She said stiffly: 'I do not suffer fools gladly.'

'Not even tolerantly, or mercifully,' the hunchback said,
'and thereby you take grave risks. If they should revolt
against such treatment——'

'They will not revolt.'

'You could, perhaps, rely too much on your beauty.'

'Oh, that,' she said, and laughed. 'No, I don't rely on my
looks to make my servants completely subservient.'

112

He shrugged. 'Your are very sure of your domination. As sure as I am over something.'

'And what is that?'

'My dear, I was worried after your last visit to me, and not satisfied that you had told me the truth. You appeared to have practical knowledge of the working of my machine. How did you come by it?'

She made no answer.

'I can tell you, I think,' said Duval. 'You contrived to take the plans for the machine away from my room in Paris, and have had one made. Perhaps more than one, for you took them a long time ago. Is that true, Thérèse? Have you made these machines?'

She was very still. 'Yes.'

'How many?'

'Many.'

He shrugged his shoulders and walked to the window, and stood looking towards the lake. She watched him closely, but there was no change in her expression. When at last he turned round, he spread out his hands, as if resigning himself to the situation.

'I am sorry,' he said.

'It will not affect you, Raoul.'

'It always affects me when trust is betrayed.'

'Don't think of it like that, don't——'

'But how else can I think of it? You know, as no one else does, that there was no one in the world whom I could trust—until I met you. I should have known better than to make an exception, I should have known that if I gave my devotion to any human being, I should be hurt. But—I am in love with you, Thérèse.'

'I know, Raoul.'

'You are wondering, of course, how I managed to find you. Now I, too, have a confession to make. Some weeks ago, I followed you, and discovered where you stayed in Paris and the name under which you lived. The other day, I followed you again. It was not difficult to find where you were going, and I discovered that you visited a certain factory, near Paris. Later, that you came here, by road. I had to see you, then, and find out what was happening. So I reached here an hour

113

ago, and when I came, that young man was with you. I stood just outside the door, and heard what you were saying.'

She glanced towards the door, which led to a narrow foyer and then the passage outside.

'How did you get in?'

He spread his hands again.

'I am not greatly obstructed by locks. I have made practical use of my knowledge of engineering. So, that strange little conversation is known to me. I confess that I was sorry that you broke down so completely.'

She didn't answer.

'Now, what are you thinking?' he asked. 'Are you wondering, behind that beautiful face, how best to remove this new and unexpected danger?'

'Raoul! Don't talk like that.'

'My dear Thérèse, how else can I talk? I have always told you that I love your beauty, and believe it to be unique. But I have never been sure of your mind. There, I think, is ugliness, and you showed it just now. But the really significant thing is not that you have deceived me, but that you are deceiving yourself. That is extremely dangerous.'

'I don't understand you.'

'You should. You are pretending that you do not know the meaning of fear, but you do know it only too well. Only fear would affect you as you were affected just now. What do you fear?'

She said hardily: 'You are wrong, Raoul.'

'Then I am wrong, Thérèse,' Duval agreed. 'Now let us return to the important subject—what do you propose to do, now that I share some of your secrets?'

For a moment she was silent.

'Well?' he asked.

'I propose to do nothing,' she said at last.

'Why not?'

'Because I trust you.'

'With secrets like these? With the knowledge that you have found a way to power greater than any man or woman has ever had? With the knowledge that, using these machines as you can, you could threaten—the *world*?' His words were clear and yet his voice hardly made a sound. 'With the

114

knowledge that you have destroyed once, perhaps more than once, and will destroy again? That you seek the man Palfrey, to kill him?'

'Yes,' she said.

'My dear, I don't believe you. Perhaps at worst you will have me watched, and——'

'I shall not have you watched,' said the woman. 'I rely on you too much. I admit that when you came in I was shocked, I did not like you to see me in such a mood, although I think you have suspected my capacity for hatred.' She smiled, and put out a hand. 'But Raoul, I have been wanting to talk something over seriously with you for some time.'

He stood quite still.

'It is this,' she said. 'I cannot go on, alone, for much longer. For I *am* alone. Oh, I employ men like that fool outside; and hundreds of others. I control them, tell them what to do, and know that I can rely on their allegiance because I have found a way of conquering their minds and their individualities. But I am tired of it, Raoul; there has been only one man to talk to, for years. You. I have not been able to take others into my confidence, to talk on equal terms, to work with anyone without despising him or her. I need—a companion.'

'I see,' said Duval softly.

'I've studied you closely, Raoul. You have all the qualities that are needed. Except towards me, you are completely dispassionate and without sentiment or emotion. You have the right kind of mind, you have conceived the impossible, and have set yourself to achieve it. That is what I am doing. Raoul, I need a constant companion and a partner, with whom to talk and plan, with whom to share the burden that I've carried for a long time. You have a quality of peacefulness which I have never found in another man or woman. You could—join me.

'You could supply the only thing I need, Raoul.' He gazed at her, his eyes narrowed. 'There is only one factor that makes me hesitate.'

'What is it?'

'You are in love with me.'

He made no comment.

115

'I am not in love with you, I shall never be in love with anyone, but—I could be a wonderful companion, and we have affinity, I think, I am sure, we could give each other happiness.'

'It is—possible,' he said.

'Only that?' She turned her head, and her eyes were wide and innocent.

'When we let loose the emotions, we can never be sure where they stop.'

'Emotions? You make too much of them. For the rest, we shall have everything, Raoul.'

'Everything, except your heart.'

'I have no heart,' she said.

She turned to him, her smile deep and satisfying.

'I must talk,' she said swiftly, eagerly. 'I must tell someone what I plan to do. I tell you I must!' She took his hand and drew him nearer. 'You were quite right, Raoul, I am frightened—but not of what Palfrey or others may do. I am frightened of myself—you are right again. I am frightened that I might go mad, unless I can share everything with—you. Yes, Raoul, only with you.'

Quite suddenly, he was close to her, and then the door burst open and the young man rushed in.

'Signora, the big . . .' He saw them, and stopped abruptly.

She did not move or shift one inch of her position, but stared the youth as at something sub-human. Her voice was icy.

'Why did you interrupt?'

'Signora, I did not know, I am sorry, I would not have interrupted, but—the big Russian is in Lucerne.'

'The—*Russian*,' she breathed.

'The big man whom Palfrey met in Stockholm, who has been with him in Paris and in England, he is in Lucerne. I saw him myself, walking along the lake. There could not be another man of the same size and the same kind of face. It is the man. Is it possible that he has traced us?'

'That is quite impossible,' said the woman.

She looked at the hunchback, and found his gaze on her, questioning, searching.

Stefan Andromovitch walked past the Hotel Schweizerhof looking neither to the right or to the left. Strolling on, he

116

reached a corner restaurant and climbed the stairs to the overhanging balcony. Here he sat at a table nearest the lake. Ordering tea, he took out a pair of field-glasses and scanned the Hotel Schweizerhof.

Presently he saw a small man at the window, talking to someone within, before the shutters were pulled close. Andromovitch put his glasses down, adjusted his chair so that he could see the hotel easily, and poured out tea.

He had been sitting there for twenty minutes when he was joined by a stocky, keen-eyed man, dressed inconspicuously.

They shook hands.

'It's good to see you, Stefan,' the newcomer said in English. 'Delighted to get your message.' He lowered his voice, keeping the eagerness out of it. 'Have you seen anything?'

'The small man who went there earlier this afternoon, yes. He has just closed the shutters.'

'Did you get a good look at him?'

'My dear Muller, I shall certainly recognise him again, said Stefan. 'I took a picture.'

'Provided you don't take too many chances——'

Andromovitch shrugged.

'We need to take chances on this Albert. My plan is to be seen about the town and invite an attack. That way we might get a lead on the woman.'

'Hmm. Simple, but dangerous. And I have only a few men, one to watch the dwarf, one at the back of the hotel, to report if the woman should leave that way.'

'It will do, for now. Tell me exactly what you've seen.'

The Swiss spread his hands expressively.

'Little enough. This woman was known to have been in Paris four days ago, and therefore could not have been here then. It was not difficult to talk to my friends the hoteliers and find out what they could tell me. In all Lucerne, there was only one woman visitor called really beautiful.' He chuckled. 'They are very discerning, my hotelier friends.'

'No doubt,' said Andromovitch drily. 'What did they discern?'

'This woman arrived three days ago, and there was no indication about where she had come from. Her rooms—she has an expensive suite—had been reserved by telephone from

Paris. Also, her luggage was marked with the colour of the chalk used, that day, by the customs at the frontier.'

'You were quick.'

Muller allowed a small tinge of satisfaction to colour his expression.

'I then asked the manager if she had been here before. Yes —two or three times, and always at short notice. She is prepared to pay a fortune for the suite, and there is always one available. This time, it is the Princess Suite—Rooms 9 to 11. I should not like to know how much it has cost her, but—' He shrugged. 'Also, the same young man has always been with her, as her secretary-chauffeur; he was driving her car when they arrived. He has a separate room, next to hers but not part of the suite.

'And there was the other thing, Stefan—the dwarfs. Now the hotelier clearly remembered that when she was here before, about two months ago, she had two children with her. At least, they were dressed as children and looked like children, but talked and behaved like men. It was puzzling. They were with her only a day or two. So I telephoned Palfrey.'

'Her name?'

'It was in the coded cable which I sent afterwards to Sap, he will know it now. She says she's Italian, and is known as the Signora Madalena Bianchi.'

'And is she Italian?'

'My friend says that she is cosmopolitan—she speaks many languages, and it is impossible to be sure of her nationality. But—and this is interesting—she has received letters from London, Paris, New York, Brussels, Milan, and Lyons. I have the list. That is interesting, is it not?'

'It certainly is,' said Andromovitch grimly. 'I——'

He broke off, for he had seen a man coming away from the hotel. He did not need field-glasses to see that the man was very small; no taller than a boy. A party of tourists was standing outside the hotel, and they towered above him. He crossed the road and disappeared beneath the shade of the trees, and Muller pushed his chair back.

'I'll follow. My man watching the back of the hotel should show himself at the corner of the garden every ten minutes, and raise his hat. If he does not . . .'

'I will go and find out why,' said Andromivitch. 'Keep that dwarf in sight—there is one other man of ours following?'

'Yes.'

'Don't lose him.'

'Never!' Muller sped away.

Andromovitch stayed on the balcony, watching the hotel. After seven minutes, a man appeared at the corner of the narrow garden, took off his hat and moved out of sight.

All was well, then; the woman was still in her rooms.

Andromovitch took a tiny Leica camera from his hip pocket and fastened it into the waistband of his trousers, leaving a larger camera attached to the field-glasses slung round his neck.

He paid his bill, and waited.

Ten minutes passed, and Muller's man did not appear again.

Fifteen minutes passed.

Andromovitch left the restaurant and walked to the hotel. Here he turned into the main doors, and approached the porter.

'Signora Bianchi,' Andromovitch said pleasantly.

'But yes, sir, the first floor. I will send a message.'

'Her room?'

'I must send a message, sir, that is her request. If you will please give me your name.'

'Are there two lifts?' asked the Russian abruptly.

'Yes, sir, one quite near—' the porter pointed—'one through the lounge, and——'

'And, of course, two exits?'

'If you wish, sir, but——'

'Thank you,' said Andromovitch. 'Tell Signora Bianchi that a friend of Dr. Palfrey wishes to see her.' He strode to the nearest lift, found it already in action, and hurried up the stairs. Outside Room 9, he paused. He heard movements inside, followed by the ting of the telephone bell; the porter's message was being received.

He tapped.

A young man opened the door.

Andromovitch pushed past him. The man, astounded and frightened, backed against the wall. Andromovitch thrust

119

open the next door; the room was empty. He went across to another, and the man gasped:

'No, the Signora is——'

He might have been talking to a log of wood. Andromovitch tried the handle of the other door; it was locked. He put his shoulder to it, and the door flew open. He stepped inside a woman's bedroom.

She stood near the wardrobe, a negligée over her shoulders. He wedged a chair against the door and stood staring at her, his face impassive.

'I am the friend of Dr. Palfrey,' he said. 'You received the message, I hope.'

'Yes.'

'And perhaps I am not unwelcome,' said Andromovitch drily.

'It is the usual masculine assumption.'

'I have been anxious to see you, since you left Hilsa Island so hurriedly,' said Andromovitch. 'There were some strange events at Hilsa. Perhaps you would care to explain some of them.'

She neither moved nor spoke.

'Dr. Palfrey also wanted to meet you in Paris,' continued Andromovitch, mildly. 'Especially after the destruction of the factory, and finding the children. You have no objection to seeing him, I hope?'

'I have no desire to see this Dr. Palfrey, or to listen any longer to a madman,' she said. 'Henri!'

There was no answer.

Andromovitch said: 'I think my friends have looked after your friend, Signora. There need not be fuss and difficulty, we shall just leave together, when you are dressed, and arrange to fly to London. Dr. Palfrey will be anxious to meet you at the airport—very anxious.'

She turned abruptly.

'I presume I may dress unobserved.'

'I am sorry, but that is impossible.'

'You will be more than sorry,' she said.

Andromovitch moved towards her in two swift strides, but at the some moment she fired. The tearing pain in his chest followed a second afterwards.

Henri's voice came from the other side of the door.

'Signora! Signora, are you——'

'Stay where you are, and listen. We must leave here in ten minutes. Have the car brought to the back of the hotel. We leave the luggage, taking only the papers. Have the others watch us until we are away. We drive to France, and then to Spain, changing cars frequently. Tell the others to arrange it. Do you understand?'

'Yes, yes——'

'Hurry!'

She turned and bent down over Andromovitch. Ignoring the bright red stain which was rapidly spreading over his shirt, she took the camera from his neck, and his wallet. Dressing swiftly, she then went to a cupboard and took out a small case. She carried this, with the camera, the wallet and her handbag, and opened the door.

No one was outside.

She went out quickly, and, in ten minutes to the second, was at the back entrance of the hotel, where Henri was sitting at the wheel of a powerful Packard. The car moved off.

Upstairs, there was silence in the room where Stefan Andromovitch lay. Noises came faintly into the room from the street.

The telephone bell began to ring.

It went on ringing for several seconds.

It sounded very loud.

When it stopped, a hush brooded over the room, and was suddenly broken by a faint gasp which came from the giant's lips.

His eyes flickered open as the bell rang again.

17

Experiment

ALBERT MULLER followed the hunchback as far as the station, and watched him as he made inquiries at the office. Duval was there for twenty minutes before he walked briskly to a nearby hotel. When he had disappeared, Muller turned to the second agent who had been following him.

'Keep him in sight, even if he sees you. It's vital. Be ready to go on any journey.'

'I am ready.'

'Report by cable to London, telephone if you can, keep in constant touch. And remember, he is dangerous.'

Muller jumped aboard a moving tram, and dropped off almost outside the hotel on the other side of the lake. At the back were two porters laughing and joking with one of the maids. There was no sign of the Z5 man. Muller felt sharp anxiety as he hurried towards the back door.

The maid, laughing shrilly, ran out of the gravelled courtyard among some trees and bushes bordering it, and as Muller entered the hotel, he heard her scream.

'What is it? What——'

Muller turned back. The two men were standing among the bushes, staring down in horror. He raced across and saw his fellow agent, lying on his face with his head smashed in.

Muller dashed past the porter and the liftman and ran up the stairs. As he reached the landing, he put his hand to his pocket about the handle of his gun. He found the door of the Italian woman's suite closed, took out his gun and fired at the lock. The door sagged open. He went into the empty front room, and from there into the bedroom.

Palfrey looked up from his desk in the big room at Brierly Place, as the door opened and Kennedy appeared.

'Come and sit down, old chap.'

'Thanks.' Kennedy dropped into a chair. 'What's the news from home, Sap?'

'Fair. In fact, goodish. Marion's going to pull through, thank God. They're a little worried about her right foot, but the worst is over.'

'That's fine,' said Kennedy. 'Why don't you slip down to Brett Hall for the night?'

'Don't tempt me.'

'There's no reason why you shouldn't go,' Kennedy said. 'You'll have news from Stefan and Corny as quickly there as you will anywhere else. It's a little after four, you could be home by six, and needn't get back until tomorrow afternoon. We *are* capable of ticking over while you're away,' he added with a dry smile.

Palfrey laughed.

'All right, I can take a hint. Nothing else in?'

'Routine work going steadily on. It'll take weeks to finish the search of private nursing homes and places where they might be treating those children. And even longer to have all the garages searched for spare parts and metal alloy. But it'll all be done, gradually, and there's nothing you can do to hurry it. Since the meeting of V.I.P.s, everyone's been falling over themselves to be helpful—I've never had such a stream of reports from Russia!'

Palfrey said: 'Good, so far as it goes. The trouble is it doesn't go far, or fast, enough.'

'Well, evidence is accumulating. It can have only one end.'

'Certainly, but which one?' Palfrey moved restlessly.

'All right, you don't agree,' said Kennedy good-humouredly. 'What you want is a couple of days of normal living—if you could wipe this business out of your mind for twenty-four hours, it would do you a power of good. Only way you might get halfway to that is by going and seeing Drusilla and Alexander the Second.'

'All right, I'll go,' said Palfrey. 'By the way, what's the report on Elsa and young Gustav?'

'Just come in,' said Kennedy. 'Elsa's absolutely clear. She answered an advertisement to get that job on Hilsa Island. I suppose it's just possible that she was given treatment while she was there, but nothing indicates it.'

'Hum,' said Palfrey. 'Gustav?'

'Not so good. He had a severe illness when he was seventeen. He was treated by the best doctors in Stockholm, for meningitis. It dragged on for six months, and he was another six months pulling round. From that time on, he's been perfectly normal.'

'Well, well,' murmured Palfrey.

'It's not a rare illness, you know,' Kennedy said. 'It could have been a genuine case. There's nothing to prove that he's been through this treatment.'

'Do you know the names of the doctors who looked after him?'

'They're here.' Kennedy touched the file beneath his arm.

'Thanks,' said Palfrey. He stretched out his hand for them, then picked up the telephone. In twenty minutes he was talking to Dr. Sandersson, of Stockholm, a man he had known slightly during the years when he had been in practice.

Kennedy watched him thoughtfully.

'Yes, that's all normal enough . . . Just one other thing, Sandersson—do you remember anything unusual about the early stages . . . Or the stages before the illness developed?'

There was a pause. Then:

'Yes, I'll hold on,' said Palfrey, and began to fiddle with his hair. 'Looking up records,' he said for Kennedy's benefit, and stared dreamily across at the opposite wall. 'Hallo . . . Yes, I'm here . . . Oh, there was . . . Sleepiness over a period of seven or eight days . . . Quite exceptional, yes . . . Thanks, you've been a great help.'

Palfrey added 'Goodbye', and rang off. Kennedy got up slowly.

'Same symptoms as the others,' he said jerkily.

'It looks like it. When he was seventeen—six years ago.' He broke off, abruptly. 'All right, I won't jump to conclusions, yet. Where's Gustav now?'

'At Bright's Hotel.'

'Elsa?'

'She's at the nursing home in Kensington—much better. According to the matron the trouble was due to shock over a considerable period. Why?'

'I'll take them down to Brett Hall with me,' said Palfrey.

'And risk——' began Kennedy.

Palfrey said: 'My dear chap! If Gustav is in this business, there isn't likely to be much danger where he is. His job is probably to worm his way into Z5. Let's convince him that he's succeeding. I know, I know,' he added testily, 'we're not sure of anything yet. But we can make sure.'

He telephoned Drusilla.

'Darling, I'm coming down at once, with Elsa and young Gustav. Job for you. Better send Alex to Robina's place. He'll be all right there. Can do?'

'Yes,' said Drusilla.

Palfrey called for Gustav first, and when the Swede opened the door of his room, he exclaimed: 'Palfrey!' and grabbed his arm and drew him inside. 'You have been a hell of a time, I began to think you would never come. Have you brought me something to do?'

Palfrey smiled amiably. 'Yes.'

'Wonderful! What is it?'

Palfrey said: 'There's a Norwegian girl who was on the fringe of this business—the nurse who looked after the children while they were ill. She says that she didn't know what was really happening, and thought that they were suffering from a genuine illness. I'm not quite sure whether to believe her.'

'*I'll* find out!'

'I hope so. You've an advantage—you can talk her language. There isn't all that difference between Swedish and Norwegian, is there?'

'There are differences, but not very strong ones. Anyway, I know Norwegian fairly well.'

Palfrey said: 'Good. Now take it easy, Gustav. You're young and new to this business.' He sounded very serious; it was what Gustav would expect. 'The girl is not to know that you suspect that she might have been involved. You're to go very cautiously. You'll both stay with me, in my country home, for the night. We may move on, tomorrow. There's danger in this, you know.'

Gustav shrugged.

'Ready?' asked Palfrey.

'I have a bag packed and waiting, ever since you telephoned,' said Gustav, and rushed across the room to snatch up his valise. He seemed boyishly eager; and there was no hint of the excessive maturity and the sullenness which seemed to take possession of most of the children who had been subjected to the treatment. He sat next to Palfrey, eager-eyed, paying little attention to the people in the streets.

Ten minutes later, they reached the nursing home where Elsa had been staying since the attack on Brett Hall; it was staffed by agents of Z5, and was used for special cases, never for the general public. Elsa had been warned to be ready, and was waiting.

'Dr. Palfrey, I am so anxious to leave here, I am angry with myself for my foolishness.'

'Don't worry about that—you had a rough time, a lot of people would have put up a worse show than you did.'

'But you needed my help, and——'

'That's one of the things I've come to talk about,' said Palfrey. 'I've a young Swede in the car outside—quite a nice young chap. There's just a possibility that he's involved in this business. I want you to try to remember whether you ever saw him at Hilsa Island, and—well, just learn all you can about him. All right?'

Elsa nodded, a little uncertainly.

'Shadows all gone?'

'No, not gone,' she said frankly, 'but I no longer feel that I am followed by that woman everywhere.'

'Fine,' said Palfrey. 'You'll do.'

Gustav was standing by the side of the car when they reached the street. The sun caught the top of his fair head, giving him a touch of distinction. He eyed Elsa intently—and after a moment, Palfrey saw the glint of admiration in his eyes. There was nothing in the expression of either to suggest that they had met before.

'Now we shan't be long,' said Palfrey. 'In the back, you two.'

For the first half hour of the journey, they had little to say to each other. After that they began to talk freely. Once or twice, the girl laughed. Palfrey smiled wryly as he drove on, remembering a similar journey a few days before, on just such a day and about the same time. He thrust the thought out of his mind, but by the time they reached the gates of Brett Hall he was wondering whether he was justified in taking this chance.

They reached the house itself, and everything looked quiet and attractive; they could not see the damaged part of the Hall from here. Drusilla met him at the top of the steps, greeted the youngsters warmly, and took Elsa up to her room.

Gustav was quiet and thoughtful.

'Don't forget, this could be really important,' Palfrey said to him.

'I shall remember,' said Gustav. 'But——'

'But what?'

'She is so young, so charming, and——'

'The woman responsible for much of what happened is beautiful enough to be confused with the angels,' said Palfrey drily. 'It may be important to remember it.'

'Of course I shall not forget!' Gustav said earnestly. 'I have been waiting for this chance, Dr. Palfrey, and shall always be grateful for it.'

Palfrey left the lad, and went thoughtfully downstairs. Drusilla was in the small room in the undamaged wing, where he had talked to Bruton on the night of the explosion.

It was the first time they had been alone together since he had left, and he noticed at once that Drusilla was showing signs of strain.

'Will you be able to stay for a day or two now?' she asked eagerly.

'With luck, darling. You know how it is. I didn't have much time to talk on the telephone, you'd better know what these two might be up to.' He told her briefly. 'Only you left as the Aunt Sally now,' mumbled Palfrey. 'If you'd rather I take our guests away first thing in the morning——'

'Nonsense. There isn't much I can do to help, but I ought

to be able to watch these two and tell you more about Elsa than anyone else. I'll be all right.'

Drusilla was as much a member of Z5 as he; and Palfrey knew it. She had often worked with him, sharing the dangers and anxiety, the suspense and the deep satisfaction of success. She was happier when she was working, it was better than staying at home waiting and wondering—fearing that a ring at the telephone might bring bad news. He slipped an arm round her waist, and they looked over the parkland. The sun was sinking slowly, but it was still two hours or more to dusk.

There was peace here.

'Are you any nearer the end of it?' Drusilla asked.

'No—not much. We're still probing, on the hit and hope method. Stefan's in Switzerland. Muller sent in an interesting report, and Stefan decided to look into it himself. Kennedy let rip for five minutes on the advantages of having a quiet weekend, and——'

'You're looking tired,' said Drusilla. 'Tired and drawn, my darling.'

'Nonsense! Just thoughtful.'

'I suppose you don't realise just what a strain it is,' said Drusilla.

'Have it your own way,' said Palfrey. 'I—hallo, here we go.'

It was the telephone.

He looked at the instrument with uneasiness, curiously reluctant to answer it.

The bell went on ringing.

'It might be Robina, to say she's arrived safely,' said Drusilla, brightly.

'Oh, yes, of course, so it might.'

Drusilla picked up the telephone, smiling.

'Hallo?'

She paused.

Palfrey saw her expression change.

She said: 'Hold on, please,' and lowered the receiver. 'Sap—Stefan's been shot. He's dying.'

128

18

Shadows

Palfrey followed the nurse along the wide, spotless corridors of the hospital at Lucerne, into a darkened room. A second nurse, sitting by the side of Stefan's bed, stood up from the oxygen cylinder, on its stand by the head of the bed. Through the plastic mask which covered the face, he could see the Russian clearly; the closed eyes, the pallor, the motionlessness, as if he were already dead.

Palfrey stood looking down at Stefan Andromovitch. He looked as he felt; that he was in the presence of the shadow of death. He stood there for fully three minutes, then turned away.

Outside, the nurse said: 'We are doing everything we can.'

'Yes, I'm sure.' He had already seen the doctor, and knew the condition. The bullet had not touched the heart, but had pierced the left lung. They offered little hope, and that little was based on the Russian's superb physical condition.

'We shall inform Mr. Muller of any change,' the nurse said.

'Thanks.'

Palfrey turned away; the nurse took him downstairs and out into the grounds. He stepped into a taxi, and went straight to the Hotel Schweizerhof. The police had finished at the hotel, and everything appeared to be back to normal.

Muller was upstairs, waiting for him.

'Come in, Sap.' They went across to the bedroom, and Palfrey looked round, without speaking. 'There is nothing here that is helpful—only the woman's clothes. Many of them are models, and we have sent them to Paris, hoping to find the maker. Everything that might help us to identify the man was taken away.'

'Yes,' said Palfrey.

'I have had a telephone call from my agent, who was following the hunchback. They are at the same hotel, in Lyons, where they travelled by train. The man is travelling under the name of Raoul Duval, and his passport is in good order. I have talked to Bruton, who is making the usual inquiries.'

'Not much more to be done,' said Palfrey. 'Any luck with the camera?'

'His large one was taken. The small Leica was intact, and the film is being examined, and negatives will be enlarged. I arranged for them to be delivered here, thinking you would prefer it.'

'Much better, thanks.'

'You look—tired,' Muller ventured.

'I'm all right. What train is there from Lyons to Paris tonight? Duval might have decided to go on.'

'We shall hear, the moment there is any move. Don't worry about that.' Muller raised his head sharply, and a moment later there was a tap at the outer door. 'These may be the photographs,' he said, and went out to the foyer.

Palfrey stood in the bedroom, looking down at the patch of dried blood which showed him where Stefan had lain. He did not turn round as Muller came hurrying back to the room, a note of excitement shrill in his voice.

'Sap! Look!'

He held an envelope in one hand, a photograph in the other. Palfrey saw the photograph of the woman; even in that first glimpse of it, Palfrey caught her breathless beauty, and knew that though she had shot Stefan, he had defeated her.

Muller breathed: 'How can we fail to find her, now?'

Palfrey spoke to Kennedy by telephone.

'One photograph is being flown over by a specially chartered 'plane, it's on the way now. Another will be in the first passenger aircraft, a third is being sent by ordinary mail; we have two left, here. Have it radioed to New York, and then worldwide. Have prints taken and air-mailed to all European

130

capitals. See that sufficient are printed for all of our agents to have one within forty-eight hours. Keep it *out* of the Press.'

'*Out*?' Kennedy questioned.

'Yes—emphatically so. She doesn't know we have it, and we needn't make her a present of the news. It's the first big step forward.'

'It was bought the hard way,' said Kennedy grimly. 'How's Stefan?'

Palfrey said: 'It's more than touch and go—it'll be a miracle if he pulls round. Have you heard from Drusilla?'

'She telephoned at midnight, and said that there was nothing to report, but that they were getting along famously. Anything else?'

'Yes. Telephone Corny, tell him this hunchback may start for Paris, and to have everyone in Paris alerted. He'll be informed the moment there's any move.'

'Right. What about you?'

'I shall go wherever Duval goes,' said Palfrey.

He arranged with Muller to call him if there were any news of Duval's movement from Lyons, and then went to bed, taking off his collar and tie and shoes, and loosening his clothes. He was dog tired, but his mind probed without rest or peace.

He must, however, have slept, for he awoke to find Muller standing over him with a tea tray in his hand.

Muller said: 'There was no move during the night, and Duval is still in Lyons. I shall be told, the minute he moves.'

Palfrey poured out a cup of tea.

'How's Stefan?'

'No change.'

Palfrey looked down at the photograph of the woman, and began to understand what Elsa had meant. He could understand her feeling that the woman haunted her; it was difficult to explain, but some abnormal quality showed in the picture; as if she were trying to hypnotise him.

Two messages came, two hours later. The first, from Lyons, said that Raoul Duval was now en route for Paris. The

131

second, from Bruton, reported that he had found the home of Raoul Duval the hunchback.

Duval knew quite well that he was being followed.

He took a taxi to a large café on the Boulevard de la Madeleine, had his cases taken inside, and sat at a table in the open air, watching the ceaseles stream of people and traffic. Yet the hunchback seemed to be withdrawn within himself, unaware of anything that was happening around him.

He sat, outwardly tranquil, drinking coffee and a liqueur.

At last he stood up and went into the café, talked for a moment with one of the waiters, and moved towards his cases. He could see each of his followers in a mirror. He seemed to change his mind about taking the cases, and walked towards the door which led to the stairs and the cloakroom.

From there he sidestepped to the kitchens.

Five minutes later, he was walking towards the Galeries Lafayette. He took the first taxi which offered, and not until he was inside did he tell the man where to go.

Eventually, he reached the house near the Quai de Bethune. He did not linger, but slipped quickly through the brown door into the courtyard. Inside, he turned left, as the woman had done, climbing to the third floor. There, he rang a bell. A middle-aged woman opened the door.

'I am sorry, sir, I was in the kitchen, my hands——'

'Cooking is an art, and must never be disturbed,' said Duval pleasantly, and stepped inside. 'Is Madame Thérèse at home?'

'Yes, sir—she gave orders that she must not be disturbed.'

'Tell her that Raoul Duval is here.'

The hunchback waited in the entrance of the apartment, looking at the priceless pictures on the walls, the Louis Quinze furniture, nodding as if in appreciation of its charm.

'Please come with me, sir.'

The woman whom Duval knew as Thérèse, was sitting in a room which was large and spacious, furnished with as much care and taste as the other. She did not speak until the door was shut and her maid had gone.

'So you followed me, Raoul.'

'Let us say, rather, that I knew where to find you.'

'I realised that you did.'

'You have so much on your mind, it is easy to forget small things,' said Duval. 'Why are your men following me, Thérèse?'

She moved abruptly, and her clasped hands tightened. Without speaking she went to the window, and looked through the narrowed slats of the shutters. She seemed satisfied.

'Why did you have me followed?' Duval repeated.

'You are wrong, my friend, I did not have you followed. On the contrary I intended to ask you to come to see me, so that we could take up our discussion where we left it at Lucerne. Why did you come?'

'If you didn't follow me, who——'

'The man Palfrey, obviously,' she said. 'There are moments——'

'What happened at Lucerne?'

She hesitated before answering, then at last she spoke.

'The Russian came to see me. I shot him.'

'So you shot him—just like that.'

'It was the only way I could escape.'

'Yes, I suppose it was,' he said. 'Is he dead?'

'I have not heard, but there can be little doubt.'

'You are a practised marksman?'

'There have been occasions when a certain skill was necessary. Raoul, the time has come when I must tell you everything.'

'I think perhaps it has,' murmured Duval.

'You have no concern for people, have you?' The question came out slowly, probingly. 'You are quite unemotional where they are concerned, aren't you?'

'That is true. The fate of other people no longer troubles me. I have lived through two world wars and seen the carnage brought about by men. I am not troubled because a number may be killed. At least it stills as much evil in them as good, possibly, indeed probably, more. But you wish to speak to me of the children?'

She said abruptly: 'Some years ago, a German doctor discovered a serum which when injected into children of certain ages, at first affected their minds and made them seriously ill, and then enabled them to grow as much mentally in ten weeks as is normal in ten years.'

133

'I *see*.'

'So, I have created a race of small men.'

Duval nodded.

'Some do not respond. Most do, but there is about one failure in five.' She was watching him closely. 'The failures die.'

'And so cannot talk,' said Duval.

'You understand perfectly. There are several thousand of these adult children in different countries. One of the characteristics is that they can be trained, in the ten weeks, to give absolute allegiance to me They are taught that I am the leader, and quite infallible.'

'Are you not afraid the gods will be jealous?'

She looked at him sharply. 'I brook no rivals!'

'Brave words. Beware the thunder and the lightning.'

'The man at Lucerne was one of the first successful subjects of the treatment,' she said nonchalantly.

'So, you were quite sure of him.'

'Quite sure. When I began to work on these children——'

'All boys?'

'No, there are some girls.'

'And to what use do you put the girls?'

She laughed, softly. 'My dear Raoul. Need you ask?'

'No,' said Raoul Duval. 'I need not ask now. They are adults physically and mentally, then?'

'Except in size.'

'I see. And to what use do you put the males?'

'They have countless uses. Their appearance is not greatly altered, and a child can go where adults are suspect—so they are the best spies in the world. Many of them have worked for me for six or seven years, you would be astonished how many secrets I have discovered about most of the world's affairs. It is doubtful whether even Palfrey, who has the co-operation of most governments, has so comprehensive a record of what goes on between nations. You can see, Raoul, that it puts me in a position of very great influence.'

'Power,' he said.

'Another word,' she declared. 'That is not all, of course. Many of them are trained to fly.'

'By stratospheric aircraft?'

'Yes. I have had several hundred made, and they are used for a variety of purposes. I can send a man to any part of the world with them, Raoul, wherever great experiments are being carried out. They can observe, photograph and, occasionally, mix with the people who are working on the nation's experiments. They can also——'

'I read of the damage to Palfrey's house,' said Duval. 'And there was the explosion at the factory, I read about that, too. So, these machines can carry explosives.'

She said, simply: 'There was a girl who had seen me, and I had to kill her.'

'Did you?'

'No. Even the infallible can be betrayed by circumstances.'

Duval spread his hands.

'Why did you allow the girl to see you?'

'It was unavoidable. I was experimenting on certain children of highly placed people in Europe. There was the two-fold advantage of using them in the future, and putting pressure on their parents in the present. Unfortunately I miscalculated, and one of the parents—a close friend of the Duke of Alga—consulted Palfrey, and I had no time to readjust my plans. I had several of these special children on an island near Stockholm, where the Norwegian girl worked for me, thinking it was an ordinary nursing home for serious cases. When Palfrey discovered this island, she must have described me, for the Russian, Palfrey's chief assistant, tracked me to Lucerne. It was then I killed him.'

'And now you are a fugitive.'

'Yes, but—' she shrugged. 'I can work through others, Raoul, and it will not be difficult to keep in hiding, for a while. I have used a number of men who were wanted by the police, skilled engineers and mechanics, and for safety's sake, I have had their faces altered by a brilliant young plastic surgeon, who—' she smiled—'will do anything I ask of him. I have lived in different countries under different names, there is little danger of being found out.'

'I begin to see the difficulties,' said Raoul, 'and your need of a partner. But you realise that I am now known to Palfrey. I can be of little use to you.'

'You can be of use,' said the woman. 'To live and work

135

with me, to plot and plan and perfect what I am doing. You are necessary to me.'

'To you, or to your plans?'

'To me—as a person. As a woman.'

'But you are inseparable from your plans,' said Duval. 'What are they, Thérèse? Why have you done all this, what do you intend to do?'

She said: 'I intend to destroy mankind.'

19

The Purpose

THERESE smiled faintly, as if she knew the full implications of
what she had said, and guessed that Duval might think her
mad. The secret which she had held for years was out.

She studied Duval's calm face, his smooth complexion, the
way his hair grew back from his forehead, the way his fine
brown eyes shone, the sensitive, well-cut lips. He showed no
sign of shock, might have been expecting that bald announce-
ment. Then she saw the lips curving at the corner, and the
smile which spread from them to his eyes. She leaned forward,
hands outstretched, in an eagerness which gave warmth to a
beauty so often cold.

'I believe you understand,' she said.

'Partly. What I don't understand I can admire. So, single-
handed, you have plotted the destruction of mankind. Would
it be too much to ask you why?'

'The thing you hate should be destroyed,' she said.

'A fairly widely held belief, I understand. Why do you hate
mankind?'

'My family was wiped out in two world wars. Picked off,
one by one. I won't bore you with the details, but there came
a time when the folly of it appalled me. I hated both sides,
not, perhaps, their lust to kill, but their stupidity, their inane
idiocy. And then I made a discovery, Raoul.'

'Tell me.'

'Governments are *not* responsible for wars. It is the folly,
stupidity, greed and avarice of ordinary people that causes war,
and I began to see each one as responsible for the horrors and

137

atrocities, slaughter and despair. Mankind was killing itself.'

Duval nodded, almost casually, and she went on in a low-pitched voice, the words pouring out in a flood.

'Look at the history of the world, Raoul, and realise the inevitability of all this. It will never stop, it can't stop, because human beings are what they are.'

'Yes,' said Duval, as if he agreed.

'I looked at the coloured races, steeped in squalor and even greater ignorance, races which are still primitive in spite of a veneer of civilisation, and which would take centuries to progress even as far as the Western world. They are so steeped in the habit of man to fight and trick and cheat his neighbour, that when they have progressed, where will they be? Where the white man is now—waiting to spring at each other's throats. It is sickening folly, but it is true, Raoul.'

He nodded again.

'And so I decided to end it all,' she said simply. 'To gain power and to use it. There is a feeling that the atomic bomb can destroy mankind, so it can and will, sooner or later. But some will live to fight again—and it will all be done to prove the supremacy of one ideology over another. Well, I can do better than that. I know where the atomic stock-piles are, and can destroy them. I know where the great arsenals are, too, and can destroy them. I know the secrets of nations, with all their evidence of grasping greed and sickening folly. I tell you, Raoul, that there is no hope for mankind, there will be no hope until it is destroyed, except——'

'Ah!' said Duval sharply.

'Oh, a few will be left,' she said, 'but they can be found and trained, to do exactly what they are told.'

'Are you sure you can do it?'

'Yes.'

'Why be so worried, then, about Palfrey?'

'Because I am not prepared to launch an attack yet, it will take a little time. My forces are scattered, and I have controlled everything myself. I have to be careful.'

'How long do you need?'

'Not long, now,' she said. 'Perhaps—five weeks. If I can work with someone else, I can save time.'

'And, Thérèse,' said Duval softly, 'do you see yourself as the

138

Queen of this new world rising out of the ashes of the first?'

'Perhaps.'

'Do you?'

'Yes.'

'And you are asking me to be your consort?'

'Yes,' she said.

He watched her slender throat, creamy and smooth, her eyes just visible beneath the silken lashes.

He said abruptly: 'We must first deal with Palfrey.'

'Yes,' she said, for the third time.

'*I* will deal with Palfrey,' said Duval. 'He will be at my house by now, they will have discovered where it is.'

'How——'

He laughed at her.

'From now on, you will leave some things to me,' he said. 'Thérèse—what is the oldest person on whom you have tried the serum?'

She hesitated.

'Only on children?' he asked.

'No. No, it has been tried on men, and has always failed.'

'How?'

'They've gone mad, and died.'

'Has your scientific friend tried to improve the serum, for adults?'

She began to laugh—cold, cruel laughter.

Duval said mildly: 'I see.'

'Raoul, I want you to go to my villa near Genoa—by train. I will follow by road, and be there soon after you. Professor Adenhauer is in charge, and will expect you.'

'You've told him?'

'I knew I could rely on you.'

When Duval had left the room, she stayed in her chair, but the laughter had faded, and a frown wrinkled the smooth perfection of her forehead. She heard the outer door close, then there was silence. After a while, she stood up, and rang for the maid.

Thérèse said peremptorily: 'I have to go away. Pack everything I need, I shall not be coming back here.'

'Madame!'

'You will be well paid, and need not look for another post

for a long time.' She laughed, suddenly. 'For a very long time, a very long time!'

She went on laughing.

Bruton was sitting in the lounge of the Hotel Mellin, a small establishment renowned, among the knowing ones, as a place where comfort and good food could be obtained at a reasonable price. Bruton was reading a week-old copy of the *New York Times,* one leg resting on a stool, a cigarette drooping from the corner of his mouth. As Palfrey came in, the American looked over the top of his paper. Palfrey nodded casually, as if they were on no more serious business than spending a few carefree days in Paris.

No one else was in the room.

'Come and sit down,' said Bruton. 'How's Stefan?'

'The last I heard, there was no change. You?'

'Fine. Shift your chair a little, and look over there.' Bruton pointed through the net curtains at the window. 'See that corner house?'

'Duval's?'

'Yes.'

'Has he turned up?'

'No, not yet. Apparently he lives alone, with another dwarf, a *cretin.* Has done for years.'

'Ah,' said Palfrey.

'Every policeman in Paris has been alerted for him,' said Bruton. 'So far, twenty-seven dwarfs have been brought in. Thanks to the photograph of Duval which Muller's man sent from Lyons, twenty-seven dwarfs have been released again. Four of them had been up twice, seen by different policemen. I'm beginning to wish I were a few inches taller myself.'

'You'll pass,' said Palfrey. 'What about the people who live in the adjoining house?'

'Duval owns it. Most of his neighbours live in small *appartements,* and all are beyond suspicion, though I'm having them checked more closely, of course.'

'Is anyone watching the house?'

'Four of our people.'

'I don't mean our people.'

'There might be someone at the window of a house nearby,

140

of course, but there's been no indication of it. Why?'
'We don't want to be seen going in,' said Palfrey.
'In a hurry, are you? Why not wait for him to come back?'
'And what happens if he doesn't come back?'
Bruton laughed.
'All right, Sap, in we go.'

The door was opened by the *cretin*, who stood squarely in
the doorway and held on to the door itself, as if to bar their
entry. Palfrey spoke in French, but the dwarf made no reply.
Palfrey tried again, but the little creature merely shook his
head more violently and tried to close the door.

Palfrey and Bruton brushed him aside without difficulty.

'We're not going to hurt you,' Palfrey said in careful French,
but there was no understanding in the dwarf's eyes, only the
gleam of savage hostility.

'I guess we'd better lock him in some place,' Bruton said.
'He's dangerous.'

'I think he's dumb,' said Palfrey. 'And might be deaf with
it.' He stood smiling down at the little creature, trying to
establish confidence—but suddenly Duval's only servitor
darted towards the open front door. Palfrey grabbed and
missed him, Bruton shot out a foot, and the dwarf leapt over
it. Two other Z5 men outside tried to stop him, but the dwarf
got away. In no time at all he was out of sight.

'We're doing fine,' Bruton growled. 'He'll warn Duval that
there's a reception party. It would have been better if we'd
stayed away.'

'We can overdo the caution,' Palfrey said. 'Anyone else
about, I wonder?'

They began to explore the house and the one adjoining,
which was linked by passages. They came to room after room
filled with *objets d'art,* fine paintings, cases of coins. It was
obvious that Duval collected widely, and was a connoisseur of
the arts. In the library, filled from floor to ceiling with
volumes in several languages, they found one wall which
consisted wholly of books about the universe, the planets,
inter-planetary communications, aeronautics and gases.
Palfrey found himself becoming absorbed.

Bruton was more practical.

141

'The place is like a museum,' he said. 'What about trying upstairs.'

Palfrey put a book back on the shelf and, very thoughtful and with the feeling of excitement which had seized him once before, followed Bruton up the narrow staircase towards the room which Duval had shown the woman. The door was locked. Bruton examined it, then took out a knife with a skeleton key attachment, and began to fiddle; he had the lock back in two or three minutes.

He pushed open the door, but another faced them, and in this there was no key.

'Electric control,' said Bruton in a hushed voice. 'We're getting hot, Sap.'

Palfrey felt the smooth surface of the walls. Presently the tips of his fingers slid over a very slight irregularity. He pressed, and the door began to slide open. They became aware of a red glow, as of false daylight; and then, gradually, the hanging spheres, the sun, the moon, the earth, the whole of the planetary system lay before them.

'Well, well,' breathed Palfrey. 'What have we run into now?'

Bruton didn't answer; and before either of them moved, there was a shout from downstairs.

'Sap! Sap! Be careful!'

They heard someone running softly.

20

The Face of Venus

THEY stood in the doorway, looking down, as Duval reached the landing below. Two of the Z5 men followed him, one with a gun in his hand.

'All right,' Palfrey called. 'Don't shoot.'

Duval looked up at him.

'I have been wanting to meet you for some time, Dr. Palfrey, and more than ever now. Have you been studying my future activities?'

'I've glanced at them.'

'You and your friend are the only strangers who've ever done that,' said Duval. 'While you're here, I hope you'll take a closer look.' He opened his hand as if to wave to the men following him, and something fell and broke. A thin cloud of scentless vapour rose suffocatingly as Bruton lunged forward and seized his arm.

Duval said: 'You can hold me fast if you like, but the gas will rise, and we shall soon be caught in it. Why not come in where it is safe, and forget those men? After all, you have the house surrounded and I can't get away. I think you'll be interested in what I can show you.'

Palfrey took his gun out of his pocket.

'Go downstairs,' he said.

'As you will.'

Duval shrugged and turned, but before he had taken a step forward, a little man darted from the room of the planets, and sent Palfrey's gun flying. Then he turned on Bruton and struck him savagely in the stomach. Duval turned, swift as a

143

flash, and propelled Palfrey into the room. The two dwarfs went after him. Duval pressed a button on the inside, and the sliding door closed without a sound.

Duval dismissed his henchmen and turned to Palfrey.

'Palfrey, look at the planets.' They began to move. 'You are very impressed?'

'Very,' Palfrey said, pleasantly. 'I've a young son who'd be quite enthralled.' He was thinking: is Bruton dead? The others?

'Children? Men? All have their toys.' Nothing could disturb Duval's good humour. 'Have you looked well on the face of Venus?'

'Or the Devil.'

'On the theory that the Devil is a woman,' suggested Duval. 'Perhaps. It might be so. You can go down, Palfrey, and walk round. The floor is electrified, but there will not be any danger to you, the voltage is not strong enough. You should find it fascinating, as a man of science. Each planet is operated by a magnetic pull of different strength, which makes them move at their various speeds. That is quite easy, the difficulty has been to find out what gases are actually close to the other planets, and to find a metal which will pass through all the gases without being affected. I've found one. You knew that, I believe.'

'Yes,' said Palfrey. 'I could, of course, kill you.'

'A delusion,' Duval said. 'I beg you not to try, for failure is so often humiliating.'

Palfrey walked down the steps, conscious of the other's amused gaze. He reached the floor and looked up as the planets moved slowly round.

Duval leaned against the rails.

'Isn't it ingenious?'

'It is, indeed,' said Palfrey drily, and was glad that he could keep his voice steady. 'What are you going to do with it? Export to Mars?'

'Not yet. Do you know, Palfrey, I have placed living things —flies, beetles, spiders— inside that little model of the aircraft which you can see there.' He pointed, and Palfrey saw the shining thing poised at the side of the earth. 'It is a simple fact that when I release the gases—identical with those known

144

to make up the atmosphere of the other planets—the machine flies from one to another, staying at each in turn for several minutes before it comes back to its resting place and—' he paused—'the guinea pig, shall we say, is quite healthy! On a larger scale, I think men could be sent to the planets in the same type of machine. Stand just a yard to one side—your left.'

Palfrey moved.

'Now watch,' said Duval.

He pressed another button, and the silver streak moved from planet to planet, hovering about on the surface of each before returning to the earth.

At last the model came to its final resting place, poised on the tiny dot which represented France.

'So I have finally conquered distance,' said Duval cheerfully. 'It has to be put to the test, of course, but that will be done one day.' He turned round, took something from the wall, and when he faced Palfrey again, he was wearing a small gas-mask.

Palfrey moved forward quickly, but could not make a second step; his foot was stuck to the floor; the current was stronger now. He tried to pull it up but couldn't move. He stood, with terror tearing at him, staring at the hunchback; gradually he felt himself going numb. He could see everything, but feel nothing; he did not seem to be breathing. It was as if he were seeing himself in a nightmare.

Duval took his arm and propelled him to a flight of steps.

At the summit there was a small, concealed doorway, not much higher than Palfrey's waist.

'You have to pass through here,' said Duval. 'Bend your head. It is the way Pierre came back, of course.'

Palfrey obeyed, and had a wild thought—that he was placing his head on the chopping block. He felt his knees giving way, and staggered towards the opening, unable to will himself to stand outside. His head brushed against the top, his arms dragged against the sides. A moment later, he heard a sound, and the light went out.

He wanted to shriek at the walls, to kick and shout—but could do nothing, only crouch there, helpless and terrified. He could hear himself taking shallow, panting breaths. Then he felt a sudden movement and realised that he was in a lift, going downwards at a great pace.

The lift stopped.

Almost too dazed by now to feel fear, he was aware of being pushed and pulled by the little *cretin* until he staggered into a narrow passage.

Shuffling down it, the journey seemed to take a long time, but after a while he saw the glimmerings of daylight. He found himself inside a small boathouse, on the bank of the river. From there he was pulled into a motor launch. Slipping on the companionway, grabbing wildly at the rail, he fell helplessly.

He was still lying in the gloom of the cabin when the engine started up. Dimly the voice of Duval came to him.

'Are you comfortable, Palfrey?'

Palfrey tried to speak, but could not move the muscles of his throat or mouth.

'You will be all right,' said Duval. 'This is not an experiment but a tried and tested drug, a refinement of curare, which relaxes the muscles completely but does not relax the mind. There may be something to frighten you later on, but you need not be frightened now.'

Palfrey stared at him.

'You ought to be pleased,' said Duval jocularly. 'You've been looking for this woman for long enough, and now you'll meet her.'

He bent down and pressed a needle into his prisoner's arm.

Palfrey felt sleep coming over him in waves. Fighting against it, he slipped into unconsciousness.

Duval sat on the terrace of the villa, not many miles from Genoa, and watched the Mediterranean rippling against the stony shore. The broken coastline lay untouched on either side, for this villa was on a headland which stretched far into the sea.

Footsteps sounded on the terrace.

He looked up.

'Well, Thérèse?'

She came across to him, eagerly.

'At least you've escaped!'

146

'And not alone, my dear.'

'Are you serious?'

'Palfrey is with me,' said Duval. 'I, or rather we, have been here for several hours.'

A wave of triumph and satisfaction seemed to emanate from her.

'I should have worked with you before, Raoul.'

'Most certainly, but—' he shrugged—'it was better that the suggestion should come from you.'

'How is Palfrey? I hear he is a man without fear.'

'Not now. In my experiments with gases, I've found some with unexpected potency. One, for instance, which paralyses the muscles and leaves the mind clear. Another that attacks the nervous system, and leaves one open to every imaginable kind of fear—and I have given Palfrey a small dose of each. Just enough to make sure that he loses his nerve and vigour. Shall we talk to him?'

They walked back to the villa, through a room shrouded by shutters and curtains.

Duval took out a key, unlocked a door, and stepped inside.

The room was small and dark, and the only window had been blacked out. Duval switched on the light, and they approached Palfrey. He was sitting upright in an easy chair, his eyes glittering as with fear, his hands restless on the arms of the chair.

'This is the great Dr. Palfrey, my dear,' said Duval.

Madame Thérèse raised her hands, and began to laugh; peal after peal of laughter rang through the room.

21

Dr. Palfrey Despises Himself

PALFREY stared at her . . .

Her laughter rang out, convulsing her body, her mouth was wide open, her eyes narrowed, yet nothing could hide or conceal her beauty. He had seen only the photograph and all that it promised; it had been a pale image. Colouring, features, complexion—all merged together with an unearthly loveliness.

She stopped laughing, at last. Duval stood near, small, malicious.

She said: 'The *great* Dr. Palfrey, of course! How are you, Dr. Palfrey? I can't tell you how delighted I am to see you here.'

Palfrey made no answer.

He had some control of his muscles and his movements, but no control of his nerves.

He had known what it was to be frightened a hundred times, yet had seldom felt fear so complete and tormenting as he felt now.

'Well, there he is, Thérèse—the leader of the organisation which hope to stop *us*. They didn't know what they were up against, did they?'

The woman shook her head.

'Palfrey will soon learn,' said Duval. 'He knows about the aircraft, of course, and the children—the way in which you make quite sure that they obey you. He's actually seen the treatment in progress—I'm told that one of the subjects lost his mind, while Palfrey was there. Did you know?'

'It can happen.' Madame Thérèse shrugged.

148

'But we've made improvements, haven't we?' asked Duval. 'In the past it's only worked successfully on the young, now we think it might work on the middle-aged. About your age, Palfrey.'

Palfrey felt again that demoralising stab of fear.

'Don't look worried,' said Duval. 'The early part of the process is quite painless. Isn't that so, Thérèse?'

She nodded, chuckling.

'After all, if we could have the allegiance of the great Dr. Palfrey, and thus, possession of all the secrets entrusted to him, it would help us a great deal. And think! If Palfrey responds to the treatment, he will become a different man. Returning to London to work with his Department, he will pass on to us all the information we want.'

Palfrey gasped: 'No!' What was this overwhelming fear which was shaking him?

'But why not?' asked Duval earnestly. 'When you've finished the treatment, you will no longer be a loyal Englishman. Or a loyal world citizen—isn't that what you imagine yourself to be? You will just live to serve—us.'

Palfrey muttered: 'Let me—go.'

He struggled to his feet, but there was no strength in him.

Duval, tiny and puny-looking, moved forward and pushed him back into his chair; it needed only a touch to make him fall.

'You will be the subject of one of the greatest experiments made on man,' said Duval. 'Imagine that! We've tried all kinds of methods of taking control of the human mind, and making people do exactly what we want—haven't we? Hitler tried it, Stalin has tried it—and *we* have achieved it.'

'No!' screamed Palfrey.

'Do you know, Thérèse,' said Duval, 'I think the great Dr. Palfrey is losing his nerve. It goes to show how unreliable even brave men can be. Shall we let him rest for a while?'

'Why should he rest?' asked Madame Thérèse.

'He wants to be in a calm mood when we start the treatment, surely. I'd like it to succeed. Who is the oldest person on whom you've tried it?'

'A youth of seventeen,' she said. 'It was one of the early experiments and only partly successful, but a second treatment completed the process.'

'What was his name?' asked Duval.

'Gustav, son of the Grand Duke of Nordia. He is—' she laughed again. 'He is a guest of the doctor's wife.'

Palfrey was shocked into steadiness. It did not occur to him to doubt what they said. He had a mental glimpse of Drusilla at the mercy of a robot who would do exactly what this woman told him.

He felt his tingling nerves become steady, felt that he had greater control of his muscles.

'There is a long gap between the age of seventeen and of forty odd,' mused Duval. 'I——'

Palfrey sprang at him. He steeled himself for the effort, found a sudden access of strength, and struck Duval. He sent the little man staggering back, but before he could turn towards the door, the woman had stretched out her hand and struck him across the face. He swayed. She struck him again, viciously, and the strength drained out of him.

Duval laid a hand on her arm.

'Later, Thérèse, if necessary,' he said.

She drew back, and together they left him. Palfrey heard the key turn in the lock. He stayed where he was, limp and lifeless—as weak as if he were recovering from a long and frightening illness.

Frightening.

The whole of the future stretched out in front of him, a desert of horror. He closed his eyes, trying to shut out the vision of the woman—the dwarf—the woman—the dwarf, passing in a horrific kaleidoscope.

He heard himself groan.

Somewhere, the ghost of self-control stirred, and he gritted his teeth.

He must conquer this. He must beat them. No matter what they did, he must beat them. He had been in worse spots; well, he'd been in positions of equal danger. Why should this affect him so strongly? Why? It was the methods they used, the tortuous cunning of it; the beautiful woman and the handsome little dwarf, who looked so strange when they were together.

He began to laugh—as the woman had laughed, his head right back. The cause was as crazy as hers had been, but the wild peals, in him, issued thin and cracked. It went on and

150

on, but gradually slackened; in its place came a curious gurgling sound; sobbing. *He* was sobbing. He could stand outside himself and look at the wreck of the man he was, and despise the creature sitting there.

He fought for self-control, and gained it. He sat in silence, gradually aware of voices just behind him. It was a great effort to turn his head and look at the wall—or what had been a blank wall.

It was, in fact, a sliding door, dividing this room from the next. It had slipped an inch or two back, and he could see the hunchback and the woman sitting at a table, drinking tea.

'How many of your men are here, Thérèse?'

'Eight,' she said.

'Where is the biggest group of them?'

'There are no big groups. In some places there are twenty-five, and with each group there are several aircraft. The machines can take off in a confined space, from a window or from a skylight, and are so small that storage is no difficulty.'

'Who knows where the groups are?'

Palfrey saw the woman smile, secretively.

'I do.'

'No one else?'

'No.'

'How do you give them their orders?'

'That is simple. I send them by the machines to key-points, and they are transmitted from those points by radio. There is a code of instructions, and occasionally the code is used for ordinary telephone messages.'

'Brilliant,' said Duval softly.

'I have sufficient machines and nearly enough trained pilots to begin at any time,' the woman went on, too deadly to be boastful. 'It is simply a matter of making the final plans.'

'For complete destruction?'

She did not answer immediately. Palfrey, until then incapable of normal reasoning, felt puzzled; for a moment was almost himself. He realised that what he had overheard meant that these two had not worked together for long, that the woman was the greater danger. It was she who was in supreme control.

She looked at Duval almost as if she weren't sure of him.

'Yes—don't you like the proposal, Raoul?'

'Oh, I like it! But are you sure it can be done?'

She laughed softly.

'Oh, it can be done. With Palfrey I used an ordinary explosive. When the final attack comes, I propose to use bacteria.'

'So,' breathed Duval.

'Against which I, and those I wish to serve me, have been immunised,' she said.

'You didn't tell me this.'

'There was little time to tell you everything. You will have to be immunised, Raoul. Meanwhile we must start work on Palfrey.'

She must have given some kind of signal, for the door suddenly opened, and the two little 'men' came in.

'Take him to the clinic,' said the woman.

It was hot in the grounds; baking hot. Palfrey felt the heat strike at him as he stumbled along the path. In front of him was a little 'man' who didn't come up to his waist, and behind him, another—jailers in the land of Lilliput. They had not troubled to bind his arms or to prevent him from running away, knowing that he hadn't the physical strength.

He saw the building they appeared to be making for, high on the edge of the cliff, much like the house on Hilsa Island. He remembered that house—Elsa, and the dwarf who had flung himself out of the window.

Presently they arrived. The strong fingers of his captors clutched him as a man in white approached, holding a hypodermic syringe.

22

A Message for Gustav

BRUTON stirred, and sat up. The door opened to admit a doctor who had been hurriedly summoned to the house near the river. He was one of Z5's agents, who played little active part but could always be called in an emergency like this.

'How do you feel, Corny?'

'Terrible!'

'You look it,' said the doctor, unfeelingly, 'but I don't think it'll be serious. I'm pretty sure you'll be on your legs again tomorrow.'

'Well, that's something. Doc—have they found Sap?'

The doctor shook his head.

'And the upstair room?'

'We've found a way in. It's a fantastic place, but—empty.'

Bruton said blankly: 'It *can't* be.'

'It was empty when we broke in. All the police are mobilised, and everything is being done that can be, Corny.'

Next morning Bruton felt better. But there was no news of Palfrey or the hunchback.

Drusilla heard the whang of tennis ball and racquets, but could not see Elsa or Gustav.

Bruton had telephoned late the previous night to tell her that Sap was missing. There had been a sketchy explanation from Kennedy that morning, but no news.

She heard a car coming along the drive, and recognised Bruton's gleaming Buick, low and rakish, as it hurtled towards the house. Bruton jumped out of the car at sight of her, but she could tell from his expression that he had no news.

"Lo, 'Silla!'

'No news?'

He shook his head.

'I shouldn't worry too much,' he said awkwardly. 'You can take it from me, they don't want Sap dead. He's too useful to them.'

'Useful,' said Drusilla, and closed her eyes. 'You mean they'll torture him to make him tell them what he knows.'

'He won't let himself be tortured, he'll tell them. Sure he will, 'Silla, don't let this get you down. He never was a hero for the sake of being heroic, and he can't do any harm in telling them what he knows. It wouldn't surprise me if we have word from him almost any time.'

'It would me,' said Drusilla.

He slipped an arm through hers.

'Come and fix me a drink, and pep yourself up a bit, it's after six.'

He heard Elsa laugh, and Gustav's answering chuckle. The young couple had stopped playing, and were strolling towards the gate in the high wire fence. Gustav's hand rested on the girl's arm.

'Sap sure gets some happy ideas,' said Bruton with a grin. He had to be cheerful, had to try to keep Drusilla's spirits up. 'What's going on here? Surely the accent seems to be more on love's young dream than spy catching?'

'It does seem rather like that. I think it must be one of Sap's mistakes.'

'Could be, at that.'

'I wish I knew why he'd brought them here.'

The young couple were drawing nearer now, and Drusilla kept her voice low, forcing a smile. Neither of them knew that Palfrey was missing.

Two or three minutes later, they all went into the house. Bruton busied himself at the cocktail cabinet, shaking while Gustav and Elsa, happy and relaxed, sprawled at their ease.

'Here's to happy days,' Bruton said, and sipped. 'One of you will have to give me a game before dinner, I haven't had my hand round a racquet in months. How about it, Gustav?'

'Gladly.'

'Or what about a foursome?' Bruton cocked an eye at Drusilla.

'I don't think so,' said Drusilla. She sipped her drink, and stood up. 'I must go and have a word with Martin.'

She moved towards the door, but before she left the room, the telephone bell rang.

She hated the bell.

It had so often been her only link with Palfrey and so her only link with life. It could bring good news but more often it brought bad.

Bruton moved across and lifted the receiver.

'Hallo? Bruton here.'

He paused, frowning a little.

'Sure, hold on.' He held the instrument out. 'For you, Gustav.' He shot a glance at Drusilla, then joined her as she left the room.

No one but Z5 men knew where Gustav was, and that call hadn't been from any of Palfrey's agents.

Elsa, knowing nothing of what had sprung to Bruton's mind, watched Gustav as he picked up the receiver.

'Yes, who is it?' Gustav asked abruptly, and she thought his voice sounded strange.

He listened for a few seconds.

There was a long pause. He put his free hand to his forehead and wiped off the beads of sweat.

'Yes, if I can,' he said. 'Yes.'

He rang off, and did not immediately turn round. Elsa looked at him with growing concern. When at last he faced her it was with a harsh, fierce laugh.

'What a strange chance! An old friend is in Buckingham, and would very much like me to go and see her this evening. If I can borrow a car, would you like to come?'

'I'd love to.'

Gustav laughed again, a sharp sound, without mirth.

'I had no idea that she was in England, no idea at all.'

It did not occur to Elsa to ask him how the 'friend' had found out where he was staying. It occurred to Bruton, but he let it pass. As soon as Gustav had finished on the telephone, he hurried with Drusilla to the small private exchange; there, a one-armed man named Curtis was sitting with a cigarette between his lips and a half-smile on his face, as he scribbled notes.

He looked round sardonically at Bruton and Drusilla.

'Who was it, and what did she want?' asked Bruton.

'Long lost lady friend, judging from her voice and manner. Says she found his address from his hotel. I suppose Sap didn't leave the address at the hotel, did he?'

'He did not,' said Bruton abruptly. 'Did they fix a meeting?'

'He said he'd try to get into Buckingham tonight. He didn't sound very pleased,' Curtis said, and grinned. 'Rather a setback to his little romance with Elsa.'

Bruton growled: 'Was the girl English?'

'She spoke in English, but with an accent. Scandinavian, I'd say. She called herself Hilde.'

'Where are they to meet?'

'Outside the entrance to Stowe Park—at the end of the avenue of elms,' said Curtis. 'Like me to arrange for a couple of hearties to be on the spot?'

'Yes,' said Bruton. 'I'll be there, too.'

'Of course,' said Drusilla, 'you can have the small car.'

'You are very kind,' said Gustav, formally.

Bruton left earlier than Gustav and Elsa, reaching the meeting place a little before the time arranged by Gustav and the girl who had telephoned. Bruton parked his car nearby, out of sight of the road, and stood behind some bushes, watching the road through a tracery of leaves.

Presently an open coupé came along and pulled into the side of the road. The girl in it was fair-haired, and very much a Scandinavian type. Sleek and composed, she glanced casually at each passing car.

Another car came along, and Bruton recognised the engine of Drusilla's Singer runabout. Bruton saw Gustav at the wheel, alone.

So he had dropped Elsa in the town.

One of the Z5 men whom Curtis had sent to the spot, moved

156

from his hiding place and joined Bruton as Gustav stopped in front of the girl.

'What to do, Corny?'

'Radio the make and number of the girl's car to the police, have them pass it on to Scotland Yard. Don't follow it, just make sure the car's traced so we can pick up the girl when we want to. Give them a clear description—the nearside front wing is buckled a bit, they'll spot that even if the number is changed.'

The Z5 man nodded, and moved away.

The girl had greeted Gustav, and he was now sitting in her car, straight as a post, listening, and looking ahead of him.

The girl stopped talking.

'It is impossible,' Gustav said, clearly.

'It isn't, Gustav, and you have to do it.'

Bruton had heard Gustav's words, fairly easily, but the girl's voice was pitched lower.

'I cannot do it,' Gustav said again.

'You can and will.' The girl laughed and patted his cheek. 'You know the penalty of failure and—you *must* obey.'

He didn't speak.

'After all,' said the fair-haired girl chattily, 'there are others who can be hurt, you know. The little Elsa who is at the house with you, perhaps, and——'

'No!'

'So, my dear Gustav, you care for her? Now—what were Palfrey's instructions to you? Tell me quickly.'

He hesitated, then spoke as if under some deep compulsion. He described everything that had happened, repeating word for word Palfrey's instructions to him.

She nodded, with satisfaction.

'Palfrey, then, knows very little, or he would not suspect the girl Olsen. You have your instructions clearly?'

He nodded.

'Say nothing to anyone about this affair. Make no mistake, Gustav, it will be very dangerous if you do.'

The girl nodded dismissal, and he got out of the car and stood watching as she drove towards the gates, swung round, and then disappeared along the avenue of elms. Bruton watched the youth closely, puzzled by his reaction. Gustav's

157

eyes were hard and narrowed, he looked—despairing. It was the best word Bruton could think of. Slowly, he turned back to his own car.

Bruton did not follow him, but drove fast by a short cut to Brett Hall. He reached the Hall ten minutes before the young couple. Whatever had affected Gustav was put aside, now, he seemed cheerful and gay, and completely absorbed in his companion.

The fair-haired girl was traced by the police to a house near Regents Park. Within two hours, Bruton received a message.

It was a private school for children between the ages of ten and sixteen.

23

Treatment

PALFREY thought vaguely: 'I must have been asleep.'

He lay flat on his back, his only sensation one of warm drowsiness. This was a small room, with a window set unusually high in the wall. He could hear a whispering sound, and couldn't think what it was until, after a while, it dawned on him.

'The sea!' he said aloud.

Recollection came back slowly, but there was no sense of fear or panic, only a curious lassitude and contentment.

He dropped off to sleep again, and when he came round, exactly the same thoughts drifted through his mind. He was a prisoner at the villa on the Italian Riviera, he'd recognised that when he had walked from the villa itself to this annexe; a clinic, the woman had said.

The door opened, and the doctor in the white smock came in. One of the nurses followed him into the room, and Palfrey made no protest as a hypodermic needle was thrust into his arm. He watched as they withdrew and closed the door.

He went to sleep again, but this time it was restless sleep, spasmodic, filled with vague fears, his heart racing without any known cause.

He—must—not—give—way.

Even though his nerves were at breaking point, even as he remembered how he had behaved last night——

Last night?

He had no idea how long he had been here.

He tried to sit up, but the effort was too much for him.

Dread thoughts began to flit through his mind; he imagined that he could hear screaming, and had a swift vision of the youth who had died in Stefan's hands.

Stefan; and Stefan was dying.

He writhed and sweated; the visionary terrors of his dreams faded, but fear remained. He was being subjected to a treatment which might succeed; if it did, he would become subservient to the woman. She would be able to make him betray everything and everyone for whom he had worked; could make him be false to those ideals which had helped him to endure.

Was the treatment beginning?

He would get out; he'd manage it somehow.

He glanced up at the window.

It might be in the wall of the smaller villa which dropped sheer to the sea and the rocks. He might be able to climb out. If he could kill himself, it would be a form of victory; at least it would make sure that he wasn't used as a tool in the hands of the enemies of mankind.

Enemies of mankind——

They were treating him as they had treated those children of hate. Remember that. He had to fight back. He had to trick these people somehow, had to fool them; it was no use saying that it couldn't be done, it had to be done.

But how?

He could fight against his own fears, that would be a triumph, and might give him the chance he so desperately wanted. He remembered everything that the hunchback and the woman had said; about the groups of 'men', about the number of machines that were available. And he also remembered that the hunchback had been compelled to ask questions, so he had not been entirely in the woman's confidence. The woman was—the queen. Queen of the Children of Hate. She talked about her subjects as if she had complete domination over them.

If he could kill her, he would have served his purpose.

He did not seriously think that he could get out of this situation alive, but if he could take her with him into death——

The door opened, and the woman came in.

160

Palfrey saw her first and then the hunchback.

'It is not unsuccessful, so far,' said Duval. 'He is in the second stage, and there is a reasonable chance that he will come through it.'

'What does the Professor say?' asked the woman.

'He is non-committal, as most doctors are. It is interesting, and he wants it to succeed, but he is expecting failure. In a way, it is a pity. Palfrey has a good brain.'

She didn't answer.

Kill her.

He couldn't kill her, because he couldn't move. No matter how he tried to tense his muscles, he couldn't move. The thought of getting off the bed was nonsensical, he had hardly the strength to lift one hand.

'Have you heard from Gustav?' asked the hunchback.

Gustav—Brett Hall—Elsa—Drusilla—Gustav.

'Yes,' she said.

'Has he been successful?'

'He will be,' she said carelessly. 'He is to break down, at Brett Hall, and confess to Palfrey's wife that he has been working for me. He will tell her and Z5 where to find me. They will send strong forces to attack the imaginary stronghold, and—' she shrugged, carelessly. 'There will be a stronghold, but not where they think. None of them will live, and there will be little to fear from Palfrey's fools, after that. Palfrey himself will be either a valuable servant or a helpless lunatic. Stefan Andromovitch will be dead, also Bruton.' She laughed softly.

'*No!*' Palfrey screamed; but he made no sound.

They turned away, and closed the door on him.

Bruton had not intended to stay at the Hall overnight, but changed his mind. He had a room in the same passage as Gustav and Elsa. Drusilla was in another part of the house. Z5 men were here in strength. He would take many chances but no more with Drusilla. He had a telephone in his room and, a little after midnight, lifted the receiver and called Brierly Place.

Kennedy answered him.

'Don't you ever sleep?' asked Bruton sardonically.

161

'Occasionally. Corny, there's a glimmer of light in the darkness.'

'*What's* that?' Bruton held his breath.

'Oh, not Sap, I wish to hell it were. Stefan. They say he's taken a turn for the better, and has an even chance of pulling through.'

Bruton said: 'Is that so?' He looked at a picture on the wall; a water colour of the countryside near Brett Hall. But he didn't see the picture, he saw instead an image of the giant Russian.

'Still there?' asked Kennedy.

'Oh, sure I'm here. Yes. Anything else?'

'There's a little more news about that school near Regents Park,' said Kennedy. 'All the children there are orphans. We're not raiding it yet, just watching. There are odds and ends of information from the continent, too. They've found about fifty places where parts for that infernal flying machine are made, and eight have been discovered in England. There was a big fire at a factory near Amsterdam yesterday, and examination shows traces of the alloy, it was probably an assembly plant. It looks as if they're prepared to destroy all assembly plants, if we get near them. That's about the lot. What's happening your end?'

'Nothing, yet,' said Bruton. 'Go get some sleep.'

He rang off, and remembered that he'd said much the same thing to Palfrey. He went to the window, staring out across the starlit sky and the hidden countryside. There were no houses within sight, but some way off he could see the glow of car headlights.

It was then he heard a sound at his door.

He dropped his right hand to his pocket, about his gun, and watched; but the handle didn't turn, the sound had been a faint tap. It was repeated, and he called: 'Come in,' but he didn't take his hand away from the gun.

Gustav of Nordia appeared, wearing a pair of pyjamas and one of Palfrey's silk dressing-gowns. His hair stood on end, he looked restless and scared.

'Can you spare me a little time, Mr. Bruton?'

'Sure,' said Bruton. 'Come right in.' He saw that there were no bulges in the dressing-gown pockets, nothing to suggest that

162

Gustav had a gun. 'It's bad when you can't sleep—will you have a shot of rye?'

'No, no thank you.' Gustav closed the door and came slowly across the room, stood in front of Bruton and said in a reedy voice: 'You ought—you ought to kill me.'

'Is that so?' Bruton grinned, and clapped Gustav on the shoulder. 'Maybe I'd better hear why, before I start.'

Gustav said: 'You'll—want to.'

'All right, son, I'll want to if you want me to, but in spite of my looks, I'm not the killing kind. Now, what's on your mind?'

'It's—everything.'

'That's certainly plenty,' said Bruton. 'Sit down, Gustav, and take it easy.'

'I . . . I work for that woman.'

Bruton said: 'So you do.' He had expected many things but nothing like that explosive confession. He forced his manner to show an ease and nonchalance he was far from feeling. 'How long has this been going on, son?'

'For . . . years. Since I was seventeen. She . . . made me come to see Palfrey. She told me he was in Paris.'

'That had us guessing,' Bruton said. 'Why come across with a confession now, Gustav?'

The young Swede closed his eyes, stretched out a hand as if he were appealing to be believed, and said harshly:

'There are some things I cannot do.'

'Such as?'

'They want me—to deliver—Elsa to them.'

'I see,' said Bruton, slowly. He was feeling his way, weighing the chances of truth or falsehood, inclined at last to believe in this confession. He knew something of the influence which the woman had on the minds of her subjects, and Gustav seemed to be fighting against some unseen authority of which he was desperately afraid. 'And you don't see it that way.'

'I can't . . . sacrifice Elsa. But if I don't . . . they will kill me.'

'Maybe I'll have something to say about that,' said Bruton, and his voice became surprisingly gentle. 'Do you know——'

He stopped abruptly.

'I do not know where Palfrey is,' said Gustav. 'I met . . . one of her agents . . . tonight. I was told Palfrey is a prisoner.'

'And you don't know where?'

Gustav said: 'No. No, not for certain.' His lips trembled and he began to shake. Bruton went to the small cabinet by his bed, and took out a bottle of Scotch, poured out, and took the glass across to Gustav.

'Drink,' he said.

Gustav drank it down.

'Now you'll feel better. What can you tell me about her, Gustav? Even a little could help.'

'She is . . . all powerful,' mumbled Gustav.

'Not so that you'd notice it. Can you tell me where we might find her?'

Gustav didn't speak.

'It's important,' Bruton said, as if he were speaking to a child. 'You don't know how important.'

'I . . . I daren't tell you, she'd find out, she——'

'Where is it, Gustav?'

Gustav said: 'Near . . . Madrid. She . . . she does not work alone. She has . . . another . . . woman . . . with her.'

'Well, well,' breathed Bruton. 'Name?'

'Juanita Melano.' Gustav drew a deep breath. 'She has a big house, on a hill. A house with a red roof. Bruton, if she knows I've betrayed her——'

'She won't know,' said Bruton briskly.

He went to the telephone, and as he lifted the receiver, saw Gustav fall.

24

The Kindly Face

PALFREY lay in bed, unable to move, though fully conscious of everything that was going on about him, even of the passage of time.

It was a whole day since he had heard Duval and the woman talking about the plan they were about to put into operation through Gustav of Nordia.

The doctor came in at regular intervals, and gave injections. He had gentle hands, and a rather sad, elderly face. His eyes were unrevealing and withdrawn, but once or twice he looked down at Palfrey, and smiled.

It was now nearly forty-eight hours since he had learned what the woman planned for the agents of Z5.

He could think about it almost dispassionately between bouts of fever. He knew that the trick Gustav was to play would probably succeed.

Bruton would be careful, of course, but——

If Stefan had been free and working, Palfrey would have felt that there was more hope. He could say and think what he liked, but Stefan was the better of the two men so far as Z5 was concerned; and Corny had always admitted it.

How long would it be before the plot began to work?

For all he knew, Gustav had talked already, and the move had started.

Bruton wouldn't concentrate all his men; he'd leave some, a kind of skeleton staff. But he would regard it as a Z5 job, and rightly. He would call the agents in from all over the world, they were probably flying to assembly points, now. It would take a few days before he could strike. Of course, the place where they believed the woman to be would be watched, and doubtless she would lay a clever, false trail to make it apparent that she was there. How she would do that didn't matter.

And he—Sap Palfrey?

He lay rigid, staring at the ceiling, lapsing into periods of unconsciousness. Hard, sour, vengeful faces floated over him —and the kindly face of the doctor. Those tired grey eyes seemed to hover in front of Palfrey's, even when the man wasn't there.

He was no longer so frightened.

In his clear thinking moments, he wondered about that, and decided that it was because they had done everything they could, now, and he could do nothing to prevent them from finishing the experiment; it was a kind of resignation. The thought of madness and death had lost its terror.

He slept, fitfully, through the third night.

When he woke it was daylight. He could see the slits of brightness beyond the shutters. He lay and looked at the window.

He had come through.

What was the effect of it?

He wasn't mad. So, it hadn't affected him in the way it had some of the children. What of his mind? He was conscious of no change, thought of being disloyal to Bruton, Drusilla, his fellow-agents, was laughable. Thought of giving allegiance to the woman Thérèse was just as ridiculous; so he did not think that it had affected his mind as they had hoped.

Two nurses came in, took his temperature, and went out again. He lay back on the pillows, glancing at the door from time to time, thinking it was opening, but when it did open he was fooled; for the doctor stood at the foot of the bed before he realised that the man was in the room.

The doctor smiled; there was no doubt about that.

'You are better?' His voice had a guttural note.

Palfrey whispered: 'Yes, yes.'

'You *are* better. The treatment has been—a complete success. Complete.'

The smile was still there, but the expression was compelling. The voice dropped, and became low and forceful.

166

'I hope you understand, Dr. Palfrey, a *complete* success. I have reported that to Madame. She will expect you to do exactly what she says, she will expect you to have different ideas, to cringe, to—' he shrugged—'to worship.'

Palfrey stared at him.

'She will not, of course, expect much from you at first, but she will expect to find that you have given up all hatred of her,' said the doctor. 'You understand? Much depends on how you act now, Dr. Palfrey—your life, mine—' he shrugged, as if that were unimportant—'and the lives of many others, perhaps of millions of others.'

He seemed only to breathe the words, but they reached Palfrey's ears clearly. He didn't miss a syllable.

'You do understand?'

'Yes,' said Palfrey hoarsely.

'It will be a little while before you are physically strong again, but the weakness will soon pass. Even so, the difficulties will then be greater. Much greater.'

Palfrey said: 'Yes. Yes, but—doctor!'

'What is it?'

'They were to . . . lay a false . . . trail. Get my men, my agents, to——'

'A house in Spain,' said the doctor.

'You know where?' Palfrey found himself panting, as if he had been through a great physical exertion. 'Are they——'

'They are gathering,' said the doctor.

'She . . . will kill them!'

'It is possible. But even if your friends fail, will that matter so much? There are others, there is mankind. Dr. Palfrey, you must not show Madame that you remember and resent this plan, you must approve of all she says and does. If she thinks for a moment that anything is wrong, she will kill you. There will be no second chance of defeating her, if you should die.'

Palfrey said: 'I understand.'

The doctor smiled briefly and turned away.

Palfrey lay for some time, hardly able to think, aware only of a feeling of exultation, of deep awe and thankfulness that the means of fighting evil had been given back to him.

He had to get news to Bruton.

There would be someone at Brierly Place; Kennedy himself

167

never left, it was his job to stay at the house, day in day out. Kennedy would be there, and would be able to get in touch with Bruton almost as quickly as he could telephone a London number. One word of warning to Bruton, and one tragedy could be averted. One word.

The woman came in, alone; gracious, this time, and reassuring.

'You look better, Dr. Palfrey.'

'I—I am better.'

'You have been gravely ill, but the doctor tells me that you are out of danger now.'

'I—I feel it.'

It was easy enough to keep his voice low, because there was no strength in it, but he was terrified in case his eyes should reflect what he was feeling.

He watched her until the door had closed and he was sure that she was not coming back. He felt worse now than at any time since he had come round, it was as if he had been talking to something corrupt; beauty that was obscene.

Madame Thérèse left Palfrey's room and walked with quick, elated steps in search of Duval. He was sitting at a desk, examining a large globe.

She went across to him, with a little laugh of pure triumph.

'We have Palfrey! The great Palfrey humbled for ever.'

Duval stood up, slowly, rubbing his hands.

'So. We have everything.'

'How are you getting on?' she asked.

'We should be able to strike in three weeks.'

'Three, at most,' she said. 'Palfrey will be able to escape in ten or twelve days. We can then find out from him whether his friends have discovered anything that matters, whether they have the strength or the knowledge to stop us. Before we act, that is essential.'

'Bruton——' began Duval.

She said: 'Bruton is in the house in Madrid which I compelled Juanita Melano to let me use by threatening harm to her children. There he will find all the evidence to suggest that it is my headquarters.'

'You know, Thérèse,' said Duval, looking up at her, 'you must be quite the most ruthlessly brilliant woman who has ever lived. Now I've seen your plans, know how widespread the groups are, I am——'

'Appalled?' she suggested.

'With a part of my mind, yes. And with another, filled with admiration!' Duval laughed. 'Everything is planned to the last detail. Supplies of the bacteria gas are being sent to every group, the bombs are being prepared. There's only one thing you haven't committed to paper.'

'And that?'

'The bacteria—what is it?'

'It will cause epidemics which will make the black plague seem trifling,' she said, 'and there is an added constituent, Raoul—it will prevent putrefaction. Yes, I think of everything.'

'Will it affect animals?'

'Every living thing, except plant life.'

'That explains the fact that you have so many groups on farms and in country districts. Some domestic animals have been inoculated?'

'I have seen to it that there will be sufficient left for us to live comfortably,' said the woman. She moved towards him with her eyes blazing. She was quivering as if an electric current were passing through her body, and her face was that of a woman transformed with ecstasy.

'It is going to succeed, Raoul,' she whispered.

'Of course, my dear.'

'Think of it! A whole imbecilic world of men—dead. Then we can breed a perfect race, and you and I can rule them. *Rule* them. Raoul, do you understand what is happening, what I've done?'

He took her right hand, raised it to his lips, and bowed in obeisance.

Palfrey twisted and turned in his agony of mind. Could the doctor get word through to Bruton? Just one short sentence?

The house on the hill just outside Madrid commanded a wonderful view of the city and of the countryside beyond. Over it the sun burned with a scorching heat.

169

The house was built in the grand style, with tall towers and the rococo architecture of the East. The gardens were ablaze with flowers which had a short, fierce life and faded only to be replaced by others.

Beneath trees on the hillside, in holes dug in the earth during the night, everywhere they could find cover, were Palfrey's men. Bruton had called for some help from the Spanish Government, but proposed to make the attack with his own agents; as Palfrey would have done. He stood in the shadow of a natural cave with a pair of field-glasses in position, watching.

She was there.

Palfrey might be there.

Bruton had tested everything thoroughly, leaving no scope for mistake. He could have looked for years, without the information from Gustav, and not found this house. It was comparatively isolated, a good place to attack and equally good to defend. He had been to inordinate trouble to make sure that no one suspected what he planned to do at dusk. His men had moved in after dark the previous night. All were eager to swing into action at zero hour.

It was now nearly three o'clock, the worst time of the day for heat. Bruton glanced at his watch.

Zero hour was a little over four hours off.

With luck, he would have complete control of the house within thirty minutes of the raid. If Palfrey were there, Palfrey would soon be free. He had weighed up Palfrey's position as closely as he could, and concluded that there would be an attempt to kill him when the raid started. So, Bruton and the group with him would be first in the house. Tear gas would be used quickly and freely; with any luck they would get through without serious casualties, success depending almost entirely on surprise.

Was the woman there?

As the afternoon wore on, Bruton became more restless. He missed, and needed, Andromovitch or Palfrey, either or both of them.

He was at the mouth of the cave again, with the field-glasses at his eyes, half-an-hour before the attack was due to start.

170

25

The Dismay of Elsa Olsen

DRUSILLA heard a sound at the door, and looked up. It didn't open, and she glanced down again at the letter she was writing.

She tried to make it cheerful, because it would probably be the first that Stefan would receive. She'd learnt that morning that the Swiss doctors now considered him to be out of danger.

She heard the sound at the door again.

'Is anyone there?' she called.

The door opened, and Elsa came in.

'Hallo, Elsa.' Drusilla put down her pen. 'Come and sit with me, you're far too jumpy.'

'I can't rest,' said Elsa, and came towards the writing table. She looked older, pale, harassed. 'Will Gustav never get any better, Drusilla? Must it always be like this?'

'The doctors say that he'll be all right,' Drusilla said, trying to infuse more hope in the words than she felt. 'A collapse from nervous strain is not usually considered to be serious.'

Elsa dropped into a chair.

'I've just been to his room. He lies there and stares at me, and won't talk. I think he hates me.'

'Nonsense, Elsa! If anything, he hates himself—but he'll recover from that. If he hadn't told us what he did—' she broke off. 'Well, he tried to make amends, he has made amends.'

Elsa said: ' It's so unfair. He is so young, so—' She jumped up, and stepped to Drusilla. 'But it is *I* who am unfair! You have so much to worry you, your daughter and your husband, and you are so calm and brave. Is there any news?'

'Not yet.'

'And—your daughter?'

'She'll be all right,' said Drusilla, and remembered the surgeon's words after he had operated on Marion's crushed foot. 'I think we've saved her from being lame, but it may need another operation, perhaps two.' At least Marion was alive. And Alex. 'Try not to worry about Gustav, Elsa.'

'If he would only talk to me, I should feel better. It's as if he blames me for what he's done in the past.'

'I tell you he's blaming himself,' said Drusilla.

Elsa shook her head, and turned away, speaking in a low-pitched voice.

'Drusilla, will you go and try to make him speak? If he would say something I think he might feel better, but lying there as if he had taken a vow of silence—it's horrible.'

'I saw him only an hour ago,' said Drusilla. 'He's just the same with me as with you.'

Elsa didn't speak.

The glorious evening sunshine seemed to mock her as she looked over the garden into the parkland. Drusilla glanced at the letter:

> *Stefan, my dear, the news is wonderful. Sap told me that he insisted in believing in miracles, and was sure that you would pull through. Few of us believed him, we've been desolate.*
> *He is away again . . .*

She closed her eyes. It was very quite.

A voice, hoarse, wildly distraught, suddenly shouted: *'Get out of my way!'*

Elsa started up. 'That's—*Gustav!*'

There was a thud, followed by running footsteps. Elsa flew towards the door as it burst open, and Gustav stormed in. He was in pyjamas, had obviously jumped out of bed and rushed straight down here. Behind him, Martin hovered uncertainly.

'Gustav!' gasped Elsa.

She stood in his way, and he thrust her roughly aside. His

172

eyes were wild and his cheeks chalk white except for two spots of burning colour. His hands were clenched as he strode towards Drusilla, bare-footed, jacket open down to the waist. Elsa screamed, and Martin came running in.

'Don't worry,' Drusilla said sharply. 'What is it, Gustav?'

He stood glaring down at her, his fists raised; and she remembered what Palfrey had told her of the child who had attacked him.

'Just tell me what it is,' she said quietly. 'Sit down, and   '

'I've sent them to their death,' he said in a strangled voice. 'Bruton—his friends—all of them. I've sent them to their death.'

Drusilla's hands clenched on the table, the letter to Stefan slid across for a few inches.

'Tell me.'

'I told them—lies. Lies! That woman I met, she gave me the orders, I—had to obey. Something inside me made me obey.' He thumped his chest, and the glare in his eyes was wild, frightening. 'She told me to talk about this house in Spain, it isn't—the home—of the woman. *I tell you it isn't*! Tell Bruton, you must tell Bruton before it is too late. Tell him!'

Elsa cried: 'No, oh, no!'

'Tell Bruton!' screeched Gustav.

Drusilla stretched her hand out for the telephone, watching the wild eyes, seeing them cloud over, as Gustav turned away, groped blindly for support, swayed, and would have fallen had Elsa not grasped him and led him to the chair.

Bruton said: 'Fifteen minutes to go. Why didn't I make it earlier?'

The man with him, Garon of France, shrugged his shoulders and said drily:

'It is lighter than I hoped, we should have made it later.'

'Later, hell,' said Bruton. 'I've half a mind to be on my way right now. If Sap's there——'

'He would tell you to wait half-an-hour, not fifteen minutes,' said Garon.

There was a faint ringing sound, of the field telephone which had been run up to the cave. The man nearest picked up the

173

receiver, while Bruton stared towards the house. This would be another trifling little report, nothing of consequence.

'Corny.'

'Yes?'

'For you—Kennedy.'

'Kennedy!' exclaimed Bruton, and turned round. He snatched up the receiver. 'Bruton here.'

He listened, face set.

Kennedy said: 'We've had two messages within a few minutes of each other. The first was from Genoa, signed by Sap—it was telephoned, we couldn't be sure that it was genuine, he didn't speak himself and there was no code signal. It warned us to keep away from that Madrid house, because they're waiting for us. The other is from Gustav. Listen . . .'

Bruton didn't move.

In ten minutes, according to plan, the raid would start.

Kennedy said: 'We might ignore the first, if it stood alone, but we can't ignore it after Gustav's new version. Call it off, Corny. You've just time.'

Two parties of Z5 men moved on to the house, according to plan, because they didn't get the signal to withdraw in time. They reached the open gates of the house and entered the courtyard—and two minutes afterwards, at the time when two hundred agents should have been within the walls, an explosion destroyed the house and killed every living creature within a range of four hundred yards.

Among the dead were Juanita Melano and her children.

The doctor came into the room at the clinic, and smiled gently at Palfrey. One of the nurses was just behind him, so he did not speak, but it seemed to Palfrey that he was trying to pass on a message.

There was another of the interminable injections.

Palfrey lay quiet, with no feeling of panic but with the sense of urgency and helplessness which had been with him most of the time since he had received the doctor's first message. Not knowing what was happening outside was the worst part of the ordeal.

174

The door opened again, and the woman and the hunchback came in—both smiling.

'Good evening, Palfrey.' The woman's voice had a silken quality, matching her looks. 'The doctor reports that you are so much better that you will be able to get up tomorrow.'

'That's good,' said Palfrey. 'Fine.'

'You will be brought across to the villa, where you will have nothing to do but get well.'

'You're very—kind.'

She turned away, as if to hide an expression of triumph. But she had startled him once before by flinging out an unexpected question, as if testing him, and he was half prepared for what she said next.

'In a week you'll be in London.'

'London!'

'Yes. And they will expect a great deal from you at Brierly Place, because you see—' she paused—'most of them are dead.' She paused again, and turned to look at him as she spoke, and he steeled himself not to show the spasm of horror which this news brought.

'*All*,' he said, listlessly.

'Yes. They thought they had trapped me, and raided a castle in Spain.' The short, triumphant laugh rang out. 'We were ready for them. It happened—' she glanced at her watch—'half-an-hour ago. I had the signal just before I came in. Congratulate me, Palfrey.'

'Yes,' said Palfrey. 'It was—folly.'

'Folly?' she asked sharply.

'Folly to attempt to oppose you.'

She shot a delighted glance at Duval, came across to Palfrey, and took his hand.

'You should have realised that before, but it doesn't matter now. We think that we can use you in the new world, Palfrey, there will not be many of us, we want the best we can find. You've a little work to do in London first, and after that you can forget the past.'

Palfrey said: 'That won't be difficult.'

There was harshness in his voice, he still fought against showing his hatred for her, but if she stayed much longer she would be bound to see it. He felt the intent gaze of the hunchback, and had an almost overpowering impulse to scream. Both of them were looking at him as if they could see into his mind, read his thoughts. He clenched his hands tightly, his muscles rigid. Why didn't they go, why——

The door burst open.

'Madame!' cried Henri.

Palfrey saw the secretary for the first time—his horrified eyes and his bursting alarm.

'Madame! It has failed, there has been another message. The house was destroyed, but that is all, they—*they must have been warned.*'

Madame Thérèse stood looking at him, shocked beyond words.

Henri said wildly: 'It was Professor Adenhauer, he was away this afternoon, I saw him leaving the grounds by a side entrance. He was followed, he made a telephone call, a long distance one. It *must* have been the Professor.'

Duval cried: 'No!'

'Where *is* the Professor?' asked the woman in a quivering voice. 'Where *is* the Professor?'

'I will fetch him, Madame.' Henri turned.

'No, we will go to see him,' said Duval.

'Why?' asked Madame Thérèse abruptly.

'We should not talk about this before Palfrey,' said Duval. 'He will be excited, disappointed, it might——'

'There are moments when I wonder if you also are a fool like the rest,' said the woman fiercely. 'If the Professor did this, how can we rely on anything that he has done? How can we be sure of his treatment of Palfrey?'

Palfrey lay back, trying to drain himself of all feeling. She missed nothing; and if the doctor were made to confess——

Did it matter so much?

He would be finished, but the others were safe. Corny was alive. The doctor could have sent other news, there might soon be an attack here. He clenched his hands beneath the bed-clothes and stared towards the ceiling.

The door opened, and the doctor came in, sad, weary, but unfrightened.

'You sent for me, Madame?'

She said: 'Yes, Professor. I understand that you have been

176

out of the grounds, and that you made a telephone call to London. Is that true?'

'Yes, Madame.'

She moved swiftly, and struck him; he didn't try to evade the blow, and his smile remained.

'Whom did you telephone?'

'A house in London, Madame.'

'You—*admit that*?'

'Of course,' said the doctor. 'What use would it be to deny it?'

She struck at him again, but this time his right hand moved swiftly, he caught her wrist and held it tightly, then threw her back.

'Once is enough, Madame. You have subjected me and others to too many indignities,' said the doctor in his gentle voice. 'You have played with the minds of men and of children, you have turned Palfrey from an honest man into a rogue, you have corrupted everything you have touched because you are yourself corrupt, and—I did what I could to save others from your corruption.'

Madame Thérèse said: 'Henri, hold him.'

The doctor's smile had never been more gentle or more kindly.

'I shall tell you something more, Madame. Everything I have discovered I was able to pass on to the friends of Palfrey in London. It saved them today, and perhaps it will save them tomorrow—all the tomorrows.'

'Henri——' began the woman.

The doctor closed his eyes, drew in a sharp breath, and fell forward at her feet.

The woman drew her foot back, and kicked the dead body savagely.

'Have a guard posted in this room and outside,' she ordered Henri. 'Watch Palfrey every moment— I shall want a complete and detailed report.'

Madame Thérèse and Duval went into the room which Duval was using as an office. She dropped into a chair in an attitude of utter exhaustion. The hunchback stood watching her, then went to a cabinet, poured out a drink and took it to

177

her. She took it without looking at him.

'It is a setback, but not really a serious one,' said Duval.

'I think it's extremely serious.'

'As to that, you are too close to it to judge dispassionately. Bruton and the others are alive, certainly, and Palfrey might be suspect—though I doubt this very much. You're wise to be careful, but such a small failure does not make a great difference. The plans are ready, the enemy can have no defence because they don't know where our forces are grouped. And they don't know what weapon we're going to use. They can't even be sure that we are planning an attack on any wide scale.'

She nodded, as if she were only half-convinced.

'The Professor must have heard us talking about this raid in Spain. He couldn't possibly have obtained any further information. The room is kept locked, there are guards at the doors and the windows day and night. There's absolutely no risk of the truth being known.' Duval paused. 'The mistake was in trusting Adenhauer.'

'It was a risk, I admit. He was one of the few who have not been subjected to the treatment, but neither have I, neither have you.'

'We must decide, now, on the next move,' said Duval. 'The question being whether, or not, to start the attack before we are quite ready.'

The woman said quickly: 'But of course we must attack. We cannot risk the danger, so much greater now, of them finding us first.'

'It is for you to say. There is one important point. I cannot find in your records the group addresses in London, Paris, New York and the other big cities. These are vital, unless you are relying on the plague being passed on from person to person. It may take time to pass from the country districts to the big cities.'

'Don't be a fool,' she said testily. 'There are operational groups everywhere. I told you there were many things I didn't trust to paper. There could be failures in the country districts which would matter very little, but a failure in one of the big cities might be disastrous. We must make a clean sweep. I wonder——' she hesitated.

'Well?'

'Are we wise to strike right away? If we could be sure of another week's grace, we should be able to work on the smallest possible margin of failure. And if we could have time to find out what Z5 knows—' she broke off.

'That would mean relying on Palfrey.'

'And it may be possible. I will see Palfrey,' she decided. 'If he is safe, I think we will leave here at once and wait until he is able to report from London. If he's unreliable we'll strike now.'

'And how can you be sure?'

She laughed, carelessly, cruelly.

'I will be sure,' she said.

He turned to the door.

'I will go alone,' said the woman.

26

Decision

THE BODY of the doctor was still on the floor of Palfrey's room. Two of the little 'men' were with him, watching him lynx-eyed. It had been bad enough before, was a hundred times worse now. Occasionally he glanced at the dead man, but looked quickly away.

The woman came in.

He sensed why she had come. She motioned to the men, and they moved without a word, one on each side of Palfrey. She stood at the foot of the bed, looking at him so intently that he wanted to turn his eyes away but was compelled to look at her by some personal magnetism.

'Did you know he was a traitor?'

'No,' said Palfrey.

'Did you know he was a traitor? Tell me the truth.'

'I did not know.'

'How much did he tell you?'

'He told me nothing.'

'Had he lived, he would have told me everything. I have discovered how to make men talk. So have my servants. Did you know the truth about him?'

'No.'

'Whom do you serve?'

'You,' he said.

Sweat was breaking out on his forehead; it was hot, but not so hot as to cause that. He tried to keep himself limp, but the tight grip at his arms made that difficult. One of the men began to move his arm at an awkward angle, and pain shot through it.

'Did you know about the doctor?' The woman's voice was pitched on a low, monotonous level.

'I said no!'

'How much did you know about my organisation when you were brought here?'

'Very little, I—' he broke off, and gasped; and sweat began to run down his face.

'How did you find out what I was doing?'

'It began with Señora Melano. She was worried about her daughter. I went to see the Grand Duke of Nordia, I was followed from the airport, and—it began then.'

'Why did you choose to go to Sweden?'

'There was no reason—*oh!*' He couldn't keep back the groan, couldn't turn his gaze away from her burning eyes. 'What is the sense of this? I'm helpless, I'm telling the truth, and—I want to serve you.'

'I wonder,' she said softly. 'Why did you choose to go to Sweden?'

He felt that his arm might break at any moment.

'There were only two places to go. Stockholm—and Amsterdam. I had no special reason for deciding on Stockholm.'

'That is a lie,' said Madame Thérèse.

The other man twisted his left arm. Agony clawed each shoulder and each elbow. Sweat dropped from his forehead to the white sheet and got into his eyes, yet he continued to look at her because it was impossible to turn his head.

'Why did you choose Stockholm?'

'I tell you I don't know!'

'Had you heard about Hilsa Island, then?'

'No!'

'About me?'

'No, no! I heard about you from the man Neilssen, he caught a glimpse of you. Then—we made the raid, and Elsa Olsen was freed.'

'I had left orders that she should be killed if there was a raid.'

'The dwarf tried to kill her, and failed. He threw himself out of the window. That's all, I tell you. From there——'

'How did Andromovitch come to find me at Lucerne?'

181

'We had your description, we have a world wide organisation and the co-operation of the police. There was a report of a woman who might be you at the hotel. I wasn't free to come, Andromovitch was. He took a photograph of you.'

'How did you obtain the photograph?'

'From Andromovitch's camera, he——'

'Now I know you are lying,' she said. 'I took the camera away from you. It is in this house, now.'

'He had a Leica! In his waistband, a miniature camera. You missed that.'

He couldn't resist, the slightest movement would not ease the pain, would only increase it. Her face seemed to be going round and round, partly because of the mist in front of his eyes and the tiny beads of moisture which had gathered on his lashes.

'Is that—*true*?' He'd shaken her.

'Of course it's true. We had nothing to go on until then, except the models.'

'Did you know the truth about the doctor?'

'No!' he screamed.

'I think you did, Palfrey. Did you know that he was going to send that message?'

'I've told you—*no*.'

'Palfrey,' she said, 'I have a man in England, this Gustav of Nordia. You remember him. He was sent at my orders to come and see you, to find out how much you knew. He has had other orders, since—to mark down where your children are and to watch your wife. A word from me, and—they'll be killed. But that doesn't matter, now, does it? You give me your complete allegiance, don't you?'

He held his breath.

'Don't you?' she whispered.

He felt the pressure at one arm, but it didn't drive away the vivid images which clutched his mind.

The woman laughed.

'Release him and put him to sleep. I will deal with him later. You needn't pretend any longer, Palfrey, you still owe allegiance to the fools in London, and to your wife. Sentiment has damned you.'

When they let him go, the relief was exquisite; he hardly felt the prick of the hypodermic needle.

The woman went straight back to Duval. Judging her mood, he didn't speak.

'We shall strike as quickly as we can,' she said. 'I think we can reach all the groups by noon tomorrow. That will be the time—all of the attacks must be synchronised. We will send the orders out, then leave here.'

'So Palfrey hasn't changed, it was a failure.'

'Failure? It wasn't tried.'

'But——'

'Raoul, there are moments when I lose patience with you,' she said sharply. 'Of course it wasn't tried. The Professor experimented, but not with the serum. He gave Palfrey injections to create all the symptoms, but which were really harmless. That was the only way it could have been done.'

'Of course!' cried Duval.

'I won't risk further delay. Start sending out the messages, please—you have the code.'

'I have everything except the group addresses in the big towns.'

'I will give them to you,' she said, and began to reel off names and addresses. Now and again he had to stop her because she was going too fast, and each time she looked at him, her expression impatient, almost vicious.

Palfrey lay back with his eyes closed, and expected to feel the waves of sleep coming over him; but they did not.

Opening his eyes a fraction, he saw one of the men looking at him; he did not know whether the guard knew that he was still awake. An idea flashed into his mind, bringing the first gleam of hope. He closed his eyes again and began to breathe more evenly, as if he were sleeping. He had to struggle to keep his eyes from twitching, but knew the danger of being betrayed by his lashes.

He heard a movement. A finger touched his eye, the lid was raised, and allowed to fall.

The man spoke.

'He is unconscious.'

183

Palfrey listened intently, praying that they would go out. He thought he heard the door close, and dared to open his eyes. One man was standing by the wall, looking through a newspaper. Palfrey looked round carefully; only one man was here, the other had doubtless gone to report that he was unconscious.

He did not ask himself why the drug hadn't worked.

He coughed.

The paper rustled, and although there was no sound, he felt the guard near him. A hand touched his. The man leaned over him, and was about to touch his eyelid again. Palfrey shot out his own hand, gripped the man's wrist and twisted; the strength left in him went into that one effort, and the man fell forward, gasping. Palfrey dragged him closer, his fingers round his neck. The man struggled but was handicapped by the bed. Palfrey felt the weakness coming through him, was afraid that he couldn't keep up the pressure. The little face of the boy-man was close to his, the eyes staring, the lips slack.

The guard went limp.

Palfrey kept the pressure up for a few seconds longer, then let him go. He slid to the floor. Palfrey pushed the bedclothes back and climbed out of bed. His legs were weak and tottery, but he managed to stand upright. Then he bent down, and ran through the man's pockets. He found a small automatic and a sheathed knife. Putting the knife in his pocket and holding the gun in his right hand, he moved away.

Palfrey stood close to the wall, by the side of the door, breathing hard, praying that his strength would come back before the return of the second guard.

At last the door opened, and the other man stepped in. He glanced round, in surprise. Palfrey struck; swiftly, savagely, he went for the throat.

The dwarf slumped to the floor.

Palfrey stepped outside. The passage was empty. He heard an unexpected sound; radio music. There were lights beneath two doors. He remembered the way he had come, and reached the front door. The radio music kept him company, but no one appeared. He opened the door laboriously, shutting it

184

after him. It made a sharp click, and for a moment he waited, heart thumping. No one appeared. He stepped off the porch.

It was dark, but not entirely so. He could make out the path which led from the terrace, and the balcony over which he had wanted to throw himself. Lights glowed further ahead, from the villa itself.

Would they have guards outside the villa? Would they think that precaution necessary, or would they rely on men at the gates?

He went on, his feet leaden, every moment expecting to hear a challenging voice, or the rustle of movement as someone leapt at him out of the gloom.

He reached the villa, passing low beneath a lighted window, alert for the first shout of alarm. But none came. The sweet scent of flowers hovered about the garden, and from here he could see the calm sea and the reflected glimmering of the stars.

He reached a glass window; this was the lounge where the hunchback and the woman had sat while he had lain helpless in an ante-room. He opened the window wider, and stepped through. The door of the room was open, and there were lights in the passage. He went towards the door, and heard voices; he thought he recognised the woman's.

There was one thing he could do; kill her.

He would have to kill the hunchback, too. It was unlikely that anyone else was in the secret, they, alone, were the leaders of the organisation, and without them it would be truncated, useless.

He turned right, towards the sound of voices.

He tried the handle of a door.

He opened it an inch.

He put his right hand to his pocket and held the gun. The excitement and the strain were almost too much for him, his legs were unsteady and his fingers shaking. He had to rest. He dared not go inside until he was confident that he could shoot straight.

'And is that all?' the hunchback was asking.

'Isn't it enough?' The woman's voice was sharp. 'Send out the instructions at once, Raoul. Let it be understood that at

185

noon tomorrow they must all strike—simultaneously; not a minute earlier, not a minute later.'

The hunchback didn't speak.

Palfrey heard another sound, of someone walking towards him. He drew himself upright, and pushed the door wider. The footsteps drew nearer. He stepped inside. The hunchback and the woman sat at a table, sideways to Palfrey.

Neither of them noticed him.

The footsteps were very near, now, but he had time. He raised the gun. It wavered, he couldn't keep it steady. He tried to point it at the back of the woman's head, but knew that if he fired now, he might miss.

The footsteps were almost at the door, any moment there might be a shout of warning.

He gritted his teeth, put his left hand round his right wrist, to support the gun—and fired.

The roar of the shot, the sharp recoil, the cry of a man behind him, all happened at once. The woman jumped up, unhurt, and Duval sprang to his feet. A hand gripped Palfrey's neck, another his right arm, forcing it behind him.

The echoes of the shot faded.

Silence followed—and did not seem to be be broken even by the sound of breathing. The woman stood by her chair, stupefied, the hunchback had his hands raised a few inches above the desk.

The man holding Palfrey released him suddenly. He fell halfway between the door and the desk.

27

The Miracle

PALFREY rolled over, lay for a moment in the deathly hush, then raised his head. He thought vaguely of the knife, but that, too, had clattered to the floor. He reached his knees, and knelt, swaying. Now he saw that the man was Henri.

'Madame, are you—hurt?'

She drew a deep breath.

'No, I am not hurt. How did he get out? Where did he get the gun?'

'I have no idea, Madame, I——'

She struck at Henri's face, hitting him so hard that he reeled to one side. He pulled himself up and stood stiffly to attention.

'Go and find out! Bring the two guards to me. Bring them to me!' she screamed.

'At once.' Henri turned smartly, picked up the gun and knife and slipped them in his pocket. He reached the door, closing it behind him with hardly a sound.

Palfrey gripped the seat of the chair and hauled himself upright, swaying, but clear-headed. He saw Duval open a drawer in the desk and take out an automatic pistol; he put it in front of him.

'How did you do it, Palfrey?' the woman asked.

He said: 'I have just one thing left to do—kill you.'

'Don't be a fool,' she said, and came towards him, magnificent of face and figure, completely recovered from the shock.

'So you don't know when you're beaten,' murmured Duval. 'You have to admire his spirit, Thérèse.'

'*Admire* him, my friend? A strange word to use for hate.

187

If it hadn't been for Palfrey, there would have been no difficulties, no need to hurry, all would have come about smoothly and easily as I had planned it. Now——' She raised her hand, and the fingers were claws, the nails red, as if tipped with blood.

Her hand moved forward, slowly.

The gun was steady in Duval's fingers, and pointing at Palfrey.

'Wait for Henri, my dear,' Duval said.

'Wait?' She sprang at Palfrey's face, as the door opened.

Henri stood there.

'Well?'

'They are—dead, Madame.'

'So. That makes two less for me to kill,' she said. 'Go and get the car ready. Warn the others to be prepared to leave at a moment's notice. Double the guard at the gates and all approaches. Have the launch in readiness, in case we have to go by sea.'

'At once.' Henri hurried out.

'Is there any need for such alarm?' Duval's voice was calm and unhurried.

'I can believe anything now,' said Madame Thérèse. 'Get the messages out, Raoul, let Palfrey hear you. Tell him that by noon tomorrow a plague of death will have struck every capital in the world. By noon on the next day there will be no life left. *Do you hear, Palfrey?*'

He didn't answer.

'And when we've finished, we shall deal with you,' she said.

He was appalled by the expression in her eyes, the evil and corruption.

He was still standing a yard away from her, she was within arm's reach.

'Raoul! Start sending the orders.'

'Yes, my dear.'

If he could kill the hunchback——

No, that was impossible, he could only hope to kill her. The refrain which had been in his mind for so long, reached screaming pitch; like a gramophone record with the needle stuck. Kill her, kill her. His fingers quivered and his arms were weak, but he had to do it. Just get his fingers round her throat. When she was dead, Duval would shoot him, but—he prayed for strength to do just that one thing.

He shot his arms forward.

She had thought him helpless, and his fingers touched her throat. She tried to draw away, but his hold was too tight. He could feel her clawing at his wrists, but the expected roar of the shot didn't come. He pressed harder, but his strength was leaving him, draining away.

It was useless, he hadn't the strength of a child. He waited for the onslaught, for death, for oblivion.

He heard her say: 'Raoul!'

Then there was silence.

'*Raoul*,' she repeated.

Palfrey drew his hand across his eyes, and could see more clearly. The woman was staring at Duval, who stood behind the desk, smiling gently, covering her with the gun.

'Raoul,' she repeated. 'What——'

She broke off, as he laughed.

The hunchback, her partner, was covering her with the gun; threatening her. He had not fired at Palfrey, he was threatening the woman. It made no sense. Miracles didn't make sense.

'Raoul,' repeated the woman.

Still covering her with the gun, Duval moved from the desk to the door, closed and locked it. He passed Palfrey on the way back, and Palfrey could see him clearly now; the small and handsome face, the clear grey eyes.

'It's all over, my dear,' said Duval. 'I have everything, now —the final list of the addresses of your groups. I had to wait until I had them, I daren't act until I could make sure. It will be easy to raid these groups, as they're unprepared—won't it, Palfrey? None of them are strong, twenty-five is the strongest, according to Madame Thérèse. Do you think you have the strength to talk to your office in London, Palfrey, if I put the call through for you?'

'Raoul,' cried Madame Thérèse. 'You must be mad. You can't mean this, you and I together will——'

'You and I will do nothing more together,' said Raoul Duval. 'Yes, I loved you, but there are limits to the folly of

189

love, my dear, though less to the power of evil. I realised that in Paris, and I set out to find exactly what you were doing. I knew you were keeping back the most vital secrets, and didn't really trust me. There was one way to win your trust—to capture Palfrey. I had to fool him, too, if I'd told him and you'd tortured him, he might have betrayed me. I found that Adenhauer was revolted, too, and was able to save Palfrey— but I would have sacrified him to find these addresses. I could not act without them. I had to play with great finesse, Thérèse, I'm sure you will appreciate that. I even had to let Adenhauer die. Now—I know everything.' Still covering her with the gun in his left hand, he pulled the telephone towards him.

'Raoul don't fail me!' she cried.

Duval asked Palfrey for the number and lifted the receiver.

'Don't do it!' the woman cried.

'The call will come through soon, Palfrey. If you come here and sit down, you'll be able to speak to them. Henri will be out for some time, we should be done when he comes back.'

The woman said: 'I can't believe it. Not you, Raoul, the one man I trusted, the one man whom I felt was my equal.'

'Did you, Thérèse? I very much doubt it. There was no real prospect that you would really share life and responsibility and authority with me or anyone else. Momentarily you were frightened and needed help, but you would have recovered. Not that it would have made any difference. I could never have permitted this. The destruction of mankind wasn't in my plans. I've discovered that men are worth knowing, they're not the brutes you think, my dear. Take Palfrey and all he would sacrifice. And—he's one of millions.'

She swayed forward.

'Don't come too near,' warned Duval. 'Palfrey, can you hear me clearly?'

'Yes,' said Palfrey.

'We may not be able to get out of here, of course, Henri will probably raise the alarm, but it won't matter if that call comes through.'

The telephone bell rang.

Palfrey lifted the receiver. Both man and woman stared at him tensely. A voice sounded in his ear.

'Hallo, who's that?'

Kennedy was taking the call.

Palfrey said: 'Ken, listen. This is Sap. There's a long message —names and addresses—all to be raided at once. Ready?'

Kennedy cried: 'Yes, go on!'

Thérèse swung round towards him. He saw her coming and knew that he couldn't fend her off. She clawed at the receiver and knocked it from his grasp.

There was a sharp report, a wisp of smoke.

She gasped and drew back, her hands clutching at her breast. She stood, leaning forward, looking away from him towards the dwarf and the gun in his hand. Then, she began to collapse. As she reached the floor, the lids closed over the hideous brilliance of her eyes.

Duval said: 'Your friend will be anxious, Palfrey. Tell him this address first—the Villa Vittore, between Rapallo and Santa Markharita. Then read the others.'

Palfrey put the receiver to his ear.

'Sap, are you there?' Kennedy was crying. 'Sap——'

'All—clear,' said Palfrey with an effort. 'Now, hurry. This address first, where all the records are. Make it fast. The Villa Vittore . . .'

The telephone bell rang in Drusilla's bedroom, and woke her when she'd dropped into a fitful sleep, after hours of restlessness.

'Yes?'

'Drusilla, he's safe,' said Kennedy in a tense voice. 'We had news three hours ago. He's had a rough time, but he's safe.'

Palfrey, feeling much better but a long way from his normal self, sat in the big room at Brierly Place. It was nearly three weeks since the night at the Villa Vittore, over two since every group had been broken up, the whole fantastic race of little 'men' killed or captured, and the flying machines impounded.

Andromovitch sat back in the special armchair; he had come here by air, the previous afternoon.

Bruton sat on a corner of the big table.

A sensational meeting of V.I.P.s had just finished.

Bruton lit a cigarette.

'I wonder why Duval didn't turn up,' he said.

191

'Shyness,' suggested Andromovitch.

Bruton stubbed out a cigarette.

'When did you hear from him, Sap?'

'Yesterday afternoon—he said that he would come,' Palfrey said lazily. 'He'll turn up. Did I tell you I'd invited him to join us?'

'Will he?' asked Andromovitch.

'I don't know,' Palfrey said. 'He may decide that he'd rather retire to his planet room. Incredible chap—he fooled me completely. Undoubtedly handled it the right way, in fact, the only way. His one slice of luck—and mine—was finding an ally in Dr. Adenhauer.' Palfrey toyed with his hair. 'There isn't much we don't know. Henri let out practically everything —queer business, as soon as he knew that she was dead, he cracked up completely. Like a man without a purpose for living—almost as if he worked by clockwork, and the key was lost.'

Bruton said soberly: 'A strange woman. Let us be thankful that beauty and evil, in such an extreme degree, so seldom go together; for they nearly wrecked the world.'

The telephone bell rang.

'Hallo?'

'Duval's here, Sap,' said Kennedy.

'Oh, good! bring him up right away.'

Palfrey hurried to the door, and shook hands warmly.

'I am late, I'm afraid, but I could not face all those people, Palfrey. I've been a recluse too long. They have gone, I understand.'

'All except the odds and ends,' said Palfrey and led the way in.

Bruton said: 'The man who works miracles!'

Andromovitch stood up, and Duval looked at him, head craned backwards. He came just above the Russian's waist.

'You will, perhaps, change the name of your organisation,' Duval suggested. 'It could be called the Department of Odd Sizes.'

'So you'll join us?' Palfrey said eagerly.

'I think so, yes. It is a great privilege, and—well, I hope that I can be of use,' said Duval: 'I have certain accomplishments and advantages.'

He went to a chair and sat down, completely at ease.